The Princess That Ate Dragons

Brad D. Sibbersen

For Gary Gygax. With thanks.

And for Rachael Ray, who would love to see every unicorn punched in the face.

1

UNEMPLOYMENT SURVIVAL GUIDE

He didn't care that the boots were magical. He wasn't going to walk around looking like some damn fool elf. "What else have you got?" he asked the elderly proprietor.

"The usual. Magic sword, magic cloak, magic cauldron..."

"Magic cauldron?" repeated Neth. "What does *that* do?"

"Fill it once, and it will feed an entire village for a year!" the old man declared.

"What good is that?" Neth sneered. "Forget it. Just give me one of those potion grab-bags."

The old man selected several unmarked vials from a stack behind the counter and placed them in a holder recycled from a six pack of ale. "Buy twelve get two free?" he suggested.

"Screw you," said Neth. He threw his silver onto the floor so the old man would have to bend over to pick it up, and stormed out of the shop. Slim for a warrior, he sported very short, jet-black hair, and was clad in light chain mail. A longsword hung in a scabbard at his side. Two small sacks, tied together with a length of cord, were draped over his shoulders. One, a magical Bag of Holding that could never be filled, held the remainder of his meager belongings. A rabbit rode in the other sack, cautiously peering out as Neth strode angrily down the middle of the street.

"That was rude," said the rabbit, whose given name, or so he claimed, was Sir Hops-a-Lot. He was mostly white, but had circles of black fur around his pale blue eyes, and a few splotches of black fur on his sides and back.

"He was a crook," said Neth, holding one of the potions up so that the sun shone through it. He eyed the mixture suspiciously. "They're probably all Potions of Forgetfulness or something."

"That *would* lead to a lot of repeat business, to be sure," said the rabbit.

He makes a good point, thought Neth. He was just about to return to the shop and run the shopkeeper through when he was suddenly accosted right there on the street.

"Have you heard the Bad News?" asked an aggressively cheerful cleric in a black cloak, shoving a pamphlet in Neth's face. "The God of Darkness wants YOU..."

"Get flayed!" said Neth, shoving the cleric aside. He forgot all about the shopkeeper.

"So what now?" asked his furry companion.

"The usual, I guess. We wander around until something happens."

Besides the usual assortment of cult recruiters, beggars, thieves, and underemployed adventurers looking for trouble, the narrow streets were filled with trulls, strumpets, trollops, streetwalkers, tarts, wenches, doxies, courtesans, madams, procuresses, pimps, and panderers, many of them wanton and/or haughty. Outside of barkeeps and those in the sex trade, almost no one seemed to have a "normal" job, i.e. anything that involved manual labor, or the buying and selling of goods or services (aside from adventuring equipment, of course). It was hardly a sustainable economic model.

"You can't swing a dead you in this town without hitting half a dozen first-level idiots, Hops," grumbled Neth. Hops didn't reply. He liked to keep a low profile in crowds. Talking rabbits were uncommon (very rare, actually), and far too many people who heard him speak immediately assumed that he could grant wishes. "We need to get as far away from this place as possible," Neth continued. "These nitwits have razed the countryside for miles. I doubt there's a monster or humanoid standing within three days' ride of this cesspit."

"Perhaps we could hunker down in the next tavern and see what comes our way?" Hops chanced, keeping his voice low.

"Taverns taverns taverns!" shouted Neth, waving his arms around for emphasis. "We're forever waiting around in taverns! I'm sick of taverns! This time we're taking the initiative!" A pair of strumpets gave him a wide berth as he passed. To them he appeared to be a crazy person, shouting at himself. Neth made a beeline for the city gates.

The road out of town was lined with out-of-work adventurers. Grim, buff barbarians snarled at passers by, challenging them to fight. Wizards adorned in natty robes covered with ridiculous, meaningless symbols held handmade signs that read "Will Adventure for Food" or "No Quest Too Mundane!" An exceptionally comely female ranger was flashing men for money. There was a small pile of silver pieces on the ground at her feet.

"We're not getting out of here a moment too soon," said Neth. "The market's saturated. I might as well be back in Gnometown."

"Gnometown?" asked Hops.

"That's where I grew up," Neth explained dismissively.

"I assume it hosted a fairly large gnome population?"

"There weren't any! It was a pretty stupid name, now that I think about it."

As they left the outskirts of the city behind they spied still more of their ilk, most of them roaming around on privately owned farmland, peering into shallow caves and poking at the ground with long, cumbersome poles, looking for secret entrances. Every so often a farmer would appear and run them off, only for another party to take their place a few minutes later. "Stupid dungeon-crawlers," sneered Neth. "We're better than that." Now, too, they spied the occasional body, usually a non-human humanoid, its bones picked clean both literally and figuratively. Looting corpses could be very lucrative, of course, but after several passes by increasingly desperate adventurers there was usually nothing left to loot besides the creatures' filthy, stained underwear and maybe a few copper fillings. As they got farther away from civilization, though, they saw less and less of this – less people, less bodies, less of the bizarre flotsam and jetsam produced by their absurd occupation. Like the large mirror smashed to pieces by the side of the road that called out to them, begging them to peer into its black depths, just for a moment, or the many impromptu burial mounds that had been disturbed by grave robbers, prompting the corpses to rise as the vengeful undead, only to be put down, reburied, and disturbed once more by new grave robbers, starting the cycle all over again. Once they'd finally passed the city's furthest outpost, the keep on the borderlands, they saw no one at all. Neth took a deep, cleansing breath and looked around. It was actually kind of peaceful out here on the plains, surrounded by nothing but miles and miles of waving golden grass or wheat or whatever the hell it was. The road was only a dirt path now, and it meandered rather inefficiently, but Neth stayed true. They were in no hurry. They proceeded thusly for nearly a week, sleeping by the side of the path at night, living off the dwindling store of provisions in Neth's Bag of Holding, until, finally, something happened.

2

THE FREAKY LYNX

Hops saw it first, and smelled it, too. "Snippid, like wet leaves," he said. He was always claiming sensitivity to all sorts of obscure, invisible scents. Neth suspected that he was making most of it up. Nestled in a copse of trees, the small building was apparently a shrine. Its low stone walls, incongruously overgrown with flowering vines, extended outward to enclose a tiny garden brimming with heavily scented flowers. At the center of the garden was a marble fountain, nearly blinding in its whiteness. Crystal clear water gurgled up from the fountain's highest point and dribbled down its sides, filling a basin below. The entrance to the shrine proper was a simple archway that opened into cool darkness. Like the garden, it appeared to be entirely deserted. A good place to rest or recuperate, which meant that there was probably something horrible hiding inside. Life was tiresomely predictable sometimes.

While Hops refrained ("Snippid."), Neth chanced the water in the fountain. It was cool and delicious. He fished his water flask out of the Bag of Holding and was just about to fill it when Hops suddenly thumped the ground several times with his back foot and exclaimed "Predator!"

"You're a rabbit," said Neth dismissively. "For you, everything's a predator."

"Look out!" the rabbit squealed an instant before it landed on Neth's back. He tumbled forward into the fountain, a weight holding him down, his face underwater. Gasping for air, he elbowed the attacker off himself and rolled over onto his back. Out of the corner of his eye he spied Hops scampering off into the trees, while in front of him...

It was just a lynx. Somewhat larger than usual, and black with greyish markings instead of the more usual coloration, but other than that just a plain old wildcat. Frankly, Neth had expected far worse. It snarled as he clumsily drew his sword. He was still on his back, sprawled out in a fountain. Minor threat or no, it nevertheless had him at a slight disadvantage. But instead of attacking, it slowly backed away, hissed dramatically, then turned and ran into the darkness beyond the archway. Neth, more embarrassed than hurt, climbed to his feet. The stupid thing had probably just wanted the rabbit, and had gotten overzealous. Still, taking it out would probably be good for some experience, and besides, they were almost out of rations. You could eat cat, right? Neth didn't see why not. Sometimes he envied Hops, who could simply eat grass whenever he got hungry. That was one great thing about having Hops for a pet – he never had to buy him anything to eat. And, he reflected further, if things ever got too tight, he could always eat Hops.

"Hops!" he called out. "Where are you?" The rabbit cautiously peeped over the low wall.

"Is it gone?"

"Get over here and get into your sack. We're going in after it."

"It seems you have your pronouns confused," said Hops. "You said *we* when you clearly meant *I*. Meaning *you*."

"Fine," said Neth. "Of course, if this turns out to be the entrance to a secret underground temple, and I fall through a trap door or something and have to fight my way back to the surface, you might be alone up here for some time. Alone with all *sorts* of predators. Foxes. Hawks. Stoats. Giant, you-eating spiders. Why, *anything* could come along." Hops hesitated.

"I suppose you have a point," he acquiesced, climbing into the bag. Neth scooped up the rabbit and his other belongings. Sword at the ready, he stalked into the tiny shrine...

And found himself in a field. But it was unlike any field they had ever seen. Rough-edged, bright pink grasses, knee-high, stretched as far as they could see in every direction. The sky, which was green, had an oddly luminescent sheen to it, but there was no sun, as far as he could tell. Maybe the green was actually clouds, or mist, blotting it out?

"Ha-Nor's beard!" Neth exclaimed. It was a meaningless oath he had made up. Ha-Nor was his uncle.

"Everything smells funny here," Hops said.

"Farkas!" This was a far more common oath. "It's a farking alternate dimension." Neth was more annoyed than anything.

"So we're farked?" asked the rabbit.

"Maybe not," said Neth, looking around in hopes that the archway they'd just stepped through was still there. It wasn't. "There's always some half-assed logic to these scenarios. We'll explore the immediate surroundings, kill a few things. It'll all work out."

"If you say so."

They began walking, Neth whistling tunelessly and adopting the most casual demeanor possible, as if he were on a Sunday morning stroll to the pub. Hops, meanwhile, cautiously took in everything. There was something out there, in the pink grass, he quickly realized. Several somethings, actually. Following them, but at a safe distance. He was getting very nervous.

An hour later they came upon the lake. It was smallish, as lakes go, more of a pond with delusions of grandeur. The water had a deep purplish hue. On the far shore, directly across from them, stood the large statue of a warhorse. It appeared to be made out of some sort of dull metal. Neth craned his neck in both directions. "Looks like we'll have to go around..."

"That statue just moved," said Hops, rapidly kicking Neth's back.

"Do you always have to kick me?"

"It's instinct."

Hops was right. What they had first taken to be a metal statue was apparently a real warhorse, clad in armor. It stamped its front feet and glared at them, steam erupting from its nostrils. Quite a bit of steam, actually. Neth examined it more closely as it began to pace back and forth. Their presence was clearly agitating it.

"That's not a real horse..." he said. Indeed, what he'd assumed was armor actually covered the entire surface of the horse. It wasn't a living creature at all, or a statue. It was some kind of clockwork construct, built out of metal and polished wood, possessing some manner of uncanny, unnatural life. Its eyes glowing like two tiny red stars, it reared up, churning the air with its front hooves, and then began purposefully trotting around the lake.

"We'd better get out of here!" Hops said.

"It's a horse," Neth said, drawing his sword. "How dangerous can it be?"

"A horse killed Superman," Hops noted.

"I never know what you're talking about," said Neth. Still, the clockwork horse, half again the size of the biggest warhorse he had ever seen, did look pretty intimidating. "We'll wait until it's halfway around, and then swim across," he decided.

"What if it comes in after us?"

"If it could swim, it probably would have done so already. It seems pretty mad, and, you know, the shortest distance between two points and all that. I'm guessing that it doesn't like to get wet."

"Neither do I!" cried the rabbit. "You jump in there if you want, I'm making a run for it!" He squirmed out of his bag and propelled himself off Neth's shoulder, but Neth managed to grab him in midair.

"Oh no you don't!" he said, stuffing the rabbit back into the sack. He tied the top of the bag in a knot, trapping Hops inside.

"No!" Hops cried. "This is how they killed my sister's litter! Put 'em in a bag and threw it in the river!"

"Pipe down!" said Neth. The horse had rounded the far end of the lake and was coming towards them now.

"Please! I don't want to get wet!" Hops was begging. "I know! Put me in the Bag of Holding!"

"No! I don't want you pooping in there!"

"I won't poop in your stupid Bag of Holding!" Actually, Hops had been pooping in the Bag of Holding for several weeks, but he didn't feel it was prudent to bring that up just now.

The horse had reached their side of the lake. It stopped and pawed the ground, preparatory to charging. Neth braced himself as if he were going to face it head-on, waited until it had closed about half of the distance between them, and then bolted into the lake. Even fifty yards from shore the water was only waist-deep, but his theory held. The horse froze at the water's edge and simply stood there, staring them down with its tiny red eyes and ejecting steam from its nostrils at regular intervals. This close, Neth could hear whirring and clicking noises coming from inside it. After several moments it stamped the ground and began to trot back and forth along a small area of shoreline closest to them. It was obviously waiting for them to come out.

"'Twould make a fine mount, to be sure," Hops said sarcastically, from inside the bag. "Perhaps you can tame it and ride it, gloriously, into battle!"

"Oh shut up." Neth favored the horse with an obscene gesture and began to wade across the lake. Even at its deepest point the water was just barely above his head, so the going was easy. The horse watched from shore until they were about three-quarters of the way across, and then, snorting dramatically, resolutely trotted around the lake and positioned itself on the shore in front of them, blocking their path

"Uh-oh," said Neth. "I hadn't considered this."

"What? What?" demanded Hops from inside the sack.

"It's smarter than we thought," Neth said.

"Smarter than *you* thought, maybe."

"We'll have to go back. It obviously doesn't want us to pass, so we'll just go back to where we started and pick a different direction."

Neth waded back. The horse, snorting and stamping, watched until he was almost to shore and then trotted around the lake again, once more blocking his way. Neth turned around and tried for the far shore again. The horse trotted ahead of him and again positioned itself in his path. Instead of wading directly across, he tried for the left shore. The horse trotted to the left shore. He tried for the right shore. The horse trotted to the right shore. This went on for some time, and soon Neth's leg muscles were burning from the effort of constantly pulling his feet free from the soft mud that made up the bottom of the lake.

"Crom's moldy junk!" shouted Neth. "This is ridiculous!"

"No air..." croaked Hops melodramatically from inside his bag. It was soaked through now. "I'm dying..."

"Quiet!" snapped Neth. "I need to think."

"You'll have to face it in combat! It's the only way!"

"And be stomped to death? No thanks."

"But at least one of us can escape in the confusion! Why should two drown when only one needs to be stomped to death?" Neth considered this for a moment.

"That's it!" he finally said.

"I knew you'd see the light," said Hops. "Let me out of this bag and I'll bring back help as soon as I can, I promise!" Ignoring him, Neth locked eyes with the horse and moved ever so closer to the bank where it stood.

"You're the ugliest equine I ever saw!" Neth said. The horse snorted steam and opened its mouth. A sort of whinny that more resembled an angry, mechanical laugh came out. It pawed at the ground with one foot. Neth inched a little bit closer to the clockwork animal. "You know what you look like? You look like the result of Pegasus humping a can opener." The horse stomped its feet. Its tiny red eyes glowed brighter. For several minutes, Neth continued in this manner. He berated the horse. Taunted it. Insulted its mother. And each time he moved a little bit closer to the shore. Agitated beyond belief, the mechanical animal stamped the ground, reared up, paced angrily in tiny circles. Finally, just a few yards away now, Neth fished one of the mystery potions out of his Bag of Holding and, in one swift motion, hurled it at the mechanical monstrosity. When it shattered against the horse's metal hide, that was it. Furious beyond measure, the animal charged him... and almost immediately sank knee-deep in the soft mud of the lake bed. It managed to pull one leg free, then another, but now it hesitated to put the first leg back down, knowing that it would again be trapped in the sucking mud. It stood this way for a number of seconds, balanced on two legs, until it finally teetered over and immediately sank several inches into the muck. It continued to thrash about intermittently, but this only made it sink deeper and deeper into the sucking mud. It was like a fly in amber now. It was finished.

"A fitting fate for the thing," Neth grinned, inordinately impressed with himself. "It should not have attempted to bar our way!"

"I'm duly impressed," said Hops as Neth freed him from the bag. He didn't even seem to mind that he was soaking wet. "If you can refrain from doing or saying anything daft for the rest of the day, I might actually begin to respect you."

"As well you should," said Neth. "Now, shall we

continue our search for the missing lynx?"

"Record time," sighed Hops. Ignoring him, Neth turned and began walking away from the lake.

"Er," said Hops, "isn't this the side of the lake we *started* on?" Neth froze. With feigned casualness, he shielded his eyes and scanned the far horizon. Then he turned and looked back, across the lake. He looked to the left. He looked to the right. It was all the same, as far as the eye could see: endless, interchangeable fields of swaying pink grass.

"Farkas!" he shouted. "Damn it! Crap crap crap crap!"

"Once again, we've snatched defeat from the jaws of victory," Hops sighed.

"Can't you... *smell* the right way to go?" Neth demanded.

"It's a nose, not a compass," Hops said. "Maybe if you hadn't *stuffed me in a waterlogged bag*," he added, his tone heavily sarcastic, "I might've maintained my sense of direction."

"You'd better watch that smart mouth, rabbit," Neth said, "or come dinner time you'll *be* dinner time!" Hops flattened his ears against the top of his head and narrowed his eyes.

"Don't make me use my magical powers on you!" he hissed.

"You don't *have* any magical powers!"

"You don't know that!"

"If you had any magical powers you'd have transformed yourself into something useful by now!"

"Says the cumberground!"

"Nuisance animal!"

"Basically just a hobo with a sword..."

"Rodent!"

"I'm *not* a rodent! I'm a lagomorph!"

Neth plopped down on the bank. "So what do we do now?" he asked rhetorically.

"Pick a direction, I suppose," said Hops, giving a rabbit's best possible approximation of a shrug. "If we..."

And suddenly, instantly, it was night.

"By the gods I've gone blind!" Neth cried.

"You're not blind!" Hops assured him. "I can still see. But it did get very dark, very fast..." As they watched, two mismatched moons rapidly rose, impossibly, from two opposing horizons. The moons quickly reached fixed points in the sky and froze there. "I don't like it here!" Hops squealed. "I want to go home!"

"Stuff all this illusory nonsense!" Neth shouted, drawing his sword. "Give me something I can kill!"

As if on cue, a doorway rose from the earth in front of them. It was a simple wooden door, braced with iron supports, notable only because it couldn't possibly lead anywhere. Yet when it swung open, of its own accord, out stepped... the black lynx. Only now the mysterious cat had grown to the size of a small man. Neth grinned. The twin moons provided ample light to see his foe by; here, at last, was a problem he could solve. He readied himself as the animal padded toward him. They began to circle each other as Hops scampered out of the way. Man and cat feinted several times – the lynx with its left paw, Neth with his sword – testing one another. Then, with unexpected suddenness, the cat sprang. Neth just managed to dodge the attack, dropping to the ground and swinging wildly with his sword as the cat passed over him. Upon landing the cat spun around, hoping to take advantage of its prey's disadvantageous position, but Neth was already on his feet, and his second undisciplined swing missed the cat's nose by less than an inch. The cat hadn't expected the man to be so quick. It backpedaled and froze, one paw in the air, unsure of what to do next, and this hesitation cost it. Neth's next swing took the raised paw off clean. The creature squalled in pain as bright red blood fountained from the stub at the end of its front leg. Hissing once, defiantly, at its foe, it turned and clumsily loped off, almost immediately disappearing into the high grass and the darkness. And was it Neth's imagination, or did it shrink as it fled, the better to lose itself in the tall grass, perhaps? Hesitantly, Hops came out of hiding.

"Maybe I should keep it," Neth said, toeing the dismembered paw at his feet. "For good luck."

"That's not a myth I like to perpetuate," said Hops. "Besides, there was something unnatural about that cat."

"You think?"

"I mean it didn't *smell* like a cat. It smelled like... a person."

"Well never mind that. Look," Neth said, indicating the impossible wooden door that still stood open before them. Through it, on the other side, they could see the garden where this bizarre adventure had begun. Neth quickly scooped up the bloody paw and tossed it into his Bag of Holding.

"What if it's a trap?" asked Hops.

"If it is," said Neth, gripping his sword all the tighter, "then we shall slay it!"

"You can't slay a tra-" Hops began, but Neth had already grabbed him by the scruff of the neck and was stepping through the portal.

3

BE CAREFUL WHAT YOU WISH FOR (AND WATCH YOUR TERMINOLOGY)

The shrine and its attendant garden were not as they remembered them. The flowers were gone, the space long since given over to the wild grasses that dominated the plains. The walls were cracked and distended, the vines clinging to them brittle and long-dead. The fountain no longer functioned, and its basin was filled with dead leaves and brackish rainwater. "It was all an illusion," whispered Neth. "Bait to encourage weary travelers to rest here." He wrinkled his nose at the water in the fountain, recalling how deeply he'd drank of it.

"It has tadpoles in it," observed Hops.

"Thanks for pointing that out," muttered Neth.

"Oi, you there!" said a voice. They looked up. An old man pulling a two-wheeled cart was looking at them from the nearby path, his expression a mixture of annoyance and distrust.

"What?" asked Neth. "Are we on your lawn?"

"Not... as such," grumbled the man with the belated realization that he was being mocked. "But that shrine, that's no place to be! 'Tain't safe!" Neth puffed up with pride.

"For a commoner such as yourself perhaps not, but

I, Neth the Brave, Neth the Unyielding, have faced the beast that haunts this shrine, survived, and sorely wounded it besides!"

"Is that a fact, Neth the Blowhard?" said the old man.

"Indeed it is!" said Neth. "By way of proof, here is the creature's paw, divorced from its body by my own trusty blade!" Reaching into his Bag of Holding, Neth produced the lynx's paw and dramatically tossed it to the ground. Only when it landed on the path in front of the old man did Neth realize that, while in his possession, the severed paw had transformed into the slim hand of a human woman. His eyes wide, the old man gripped his cart tightly and hastened down the path at twice his original speed.

Neth was arrested about an hour later. The guardsmen, six of them, surrounded him on horseback just as the path again widened into a road and they appeared to be approaching a sizable city. The guardsmen asked him his name ("Neth the Blowhard!" Hops interjected before he could speak.), frisked him, and seized all of his belongings – including Hops – supplying him with a handwritten voucher for them that looked like this:

two (2) saks

one (1) sord

one (1) rabit (provisuns?)

Escorted into the city, Neth was immediately taken to an imposing, ostentatious palace, where a crowd watched with mild interest as two of the guardsmen dismounted and led him inside. "King Nomolos is renowned for his wisdom," said one of the guards. "He'll know what to do with the likes of you." Manhandled through a pair of swinging doors, Neth found himself in a smallish, windowless chamber. Flanking him, the two guards turned and stood still, quietly facing the doors they'd just entered through. Neth was about to ask what was going on when suddenly the entire chamber lurched and began to rise upward on what he would later learn was a cushion of steam. Arriving at the second floor, the guards quickly hustled Neth out of the chamber before the steam dissipated, dropping the chamber none-too-gently back to the ground floor. Before them, snaking down a wide marble staircase, was an endless line of people and humanoids of every description imaginable, all waiting to be granted audience with the King. Many of them glared as the guards, with Neth in tow, went directly to the front of the line and were immediately admitted to a gigantic throne room. Three thrones on a wide dais dominated the far end. King Nomolos – elderly but still robust, with a neat, white beard – sat on the center throne. To his left sat his daughter. She was enormous, heavily freckled, and had unpleasantly aggressive red hair. To his right sat his Queen. Slim, blonde, and quite lovely, she was also noticeably younger than the daughter.

"That's him! That's the one!" shouted a vaguely familiar voice as Neth and the guards entered. It was the old man they'd seen on the path. He gestured at Neth excitedly. "He did it! Chopped 'er hand right off, he did!" The guards maneuvered Neth next to the old man and motioned for the latter to be quiet. There were several parties in front of them, all with questions for the wise King Nomolos. Nomolos looked bored beyond comprehension as he fielded queries such as these:

"Why can't I stop spitting?"

"Am I gay?"

"Will I always be a slave?"

"Should I get my ears pinned back?" (This from an elf.)

"I have this vaginal discharge..."

"Why is 0! equal to 1?"

"Do you validate?"

Finally, it was Neth's turn. He was taken before the King by his two escorts, while a third guard set his confiscated belongings, including Hops, on the floor nearby. A fourth, less enthusiastic guard presented the severed hand as evidence, gingerly holding it with two fingers, as far away from himself as possible.

"Neth the Blowhard," announced a man reading from an important-looking scroll. He clearly was not a member of the court, but was just a little too fancy to be a commoner or a guard. A lawyer.

"Where is the owner of this hand?" asked the King, clearly disinterested. "She will have to file a formal complaint."

"Your Majesty," said Neth, dropping to one knee and bowing deeply. "Please allow me to explain the extraordinary circumstances that brought me before you today. I am Neth the Swordsman, and this," he swept his arm to indicate Hops, "is my erstwild companion..."

"'Erstwhile'," corrected Hops.

"...companion," Neth continued, annoyed, "Sir Hops-a-Lot."

"Also, *erstwhile* doesn't really make sense in this context," added Hops.

Neth's upper lip twitched. He ground his teeth.

"Oh my!" said the Queen. "A talking rabbit! How unusual!"

"Does he grant wishes?" asked the King.

"Alas, no," said Neth, quickly regaining his composure. "His practical value is... limited, at best. Your Majesty."

The King waved his hand, indicating that Neth should continue.

"Your Majesty," Neth began again, "pray ken thee 'twas not a maiden I did strike with my blade, cleaving her limb asunder! 'Twas rather..."

"In language we can *all* understand," sighed the King.

"It was a lynx," said Neth. "When I cut that hand off it was a paw, and it was attached to a lynx."

"The Witch!" exclaimed the King. There was a collective gasp. A woman towards the back of the room moaned and made a dramatic show of swooning, fully expecting her husband to catch her. He didn't. He slept on the couch that night.

"I assume there's some backstory that goes with this reaction?" Neth asked.

"Indeed," said the King solemnly. "A tale that goes back many centuries..."

"Is there a short version?" asked Hops.

"Not so long ago," the King began, "Nogard was famous for its dragons. Why, even the name of the town is *dragon* spelled backwards."

"Yes, that's very clever," deadpanned Neth.

"Our dragons, tamed over many generations, had been trained to use their super-heated breath to power steam-driven wonders! Why, a single adult dragon, directing its breath over a strategically placed pool of water, could power an entire building... with steam! Smaller dragons supplied steam for vehicles, machinery, farming equipment, even our defenses! We were the harbingers of a new age, a Steam Age! But then *she* came, the Black-Tressed Witch, the Ravenous Raveness: Princess Skylar Skylark, exiled heir to the throne of Ravendell. Using her dark powers, obtained by repeatedly copulating with the Devil (probably), she has spirited away our dragons one by one, devastating our economy and destroying our way of life. Champion after champion has set out to slay her – or at least tell her to knock it off – but her powerful illusions have felled them all. My counsel is celebrated far and wide, but even I could determine no way to thwart her. Until now, we have been utterly without hope."

"That's a shame," said Neth,

"What did you mean, 'until now'?" Hops asked hesitantly.

"You are the hero we have been waiting for!" proclaimed the King. "You, who have faced the Great Evil and escaped unscathed! You, who have drawn first blood! I hereby appoint thee to my Royal Guard! Your first assignment: slay the detestable Princess Skylar Skylark and end her predations on us once and for all!"

"That sounds dangerous," said Hops.

"Er, I'm not exactly a... 'magic' guy, if you know what I mean," said Neth, supplying gratuitous air quotes with his fingers. "And she seems to be pretty well-versed in the whole 'magic' thing..."

"For this great service," continued the King, ignoring him, "I am prepared to offer you a reward of five thousand gold..." he glanced at his royal treasurer, who all-but-imperceptibly shook his head from side to side "...five thousand *silver* pieces." The treasurer glared at him. "Before taxes, of course," the

King added hastily. "Plus, stock in our new startup, SteamWerks, LLC. It's really going places, I assure you."

"I'm honored, Your Majesty, really, but this high-level sorcery stuff is way out of my league. I'm more of a hack-and-slash type, you know? Running people through, decapitating them, that sort of thing."

"So decapitate her," shrugged the King. "In exchange for her vile head I will not only favor you with five thousand silver pieces (before taxes) but also the hand of my own beautiful daughter, the Princess Penelope."

The morbidly obese redhead smiled at him. Her teeth had strings of meat stuck in them.

"Eww," said Neth involuntarily. Hops prepared to run. The King's eyes narrowed.

"Final offer," the King said. "Bring me the witch's head, and I *won't* nail you to a tree full of bees and then set it on fire."

"I'll take it," sighed Neth.

4

ROAD TRIP!

Captain Dergar of the Nogard Royal Guard, a massive oak of a man clad in plate mail and sporting a huge, bushy mustache, had been assigned to Neth until further notice. The term being bandied about was "flight risk".

"'Dergar of the Nogard Royal Guard' is hard to say really fast," Hops pointed out as he munched on some greens that the kitchen staff had provided for him.

"Then shut up," growled Neth. Dergar would be accompanying them on their quest as the King's supervisor/enforcer. This gave Neth a modicum of hope, because despite Dergar's size Neth was pretty sure he could take him.

"The portal upon which you stumbled," Dergar was saying as he spread a map out on the table in Neth's bedchamber, "was temporary; one of many the witch uses to prey upon us from a distance! They are open only when *she* wills it, and even then they are guarded by her mind-bending illusions!" Dergar delivered every statement – even inconsequential asides like "I have to go to the bathroom!" – in a booming, self-important manner that made everything sound like a heroic proclamation. It was incredibly annoying.

"Couldn't we just plow right through the

illusions?" asked Neth. Dergar shook his head.

"Led astray by her phantasmagoria, you could fumble about in the Spaces Between the World for weeks and never travel more than a few feet in any direction! No, we must journey overland to safely reach her kingdom!" He indicated their proposed course on the map. The map had a lot of skull-and-crossbones symbols on it, Neth noted, frowning. "The most convenient path will take us over Doom Mountain, through the Swamp of the Undead, through the Relatively Pleasant Hills, and finally across the Wide Open Plains Where We're a Perfect Target! There we will find Princess Skylark's castle of sand and ice!"

"That's the most *convenient* path?"

"Yes! There are shorter routes, but it is best to avoid Unicorn Forest and Joyful Glen!"

"Fine," Neth sighed. "When do we leave?"

"On the morrow!"

"And it's just you, me, and Hops?" Neth asked, envisioning Dergar's corpse laying in a ditch alongside the road, not so very far outside the Nogard city limits. "No one else is accompanying us on this ill-advised misadventure?"

"Well, Yeth and Noe..." Dergar said.

He hadn't noticed Dergar's lisp before.

"Come again?" he said.

"Yeth and Noe," Dergar repeated. "Dwarf warriors of some repute!"

"Wait, their *names* are 'Yeth' and 'Noe'?"

"Yes!" said Dergar. "They're brothers!"

"Who's on first?" interjected Hops.

"Would you *please* keep your incomprehensible comments to yourself, you stupid, weird rabbit?" Neth snapped.

"You shall meet them in the morn!" Dergar boomed, rolling up his map. "Sleep now, and sleep well, for tomorrow we ride!" Spinning dramatically, so that his cape billowed out behind him, he marched out of the room. A bolt was thrown, locking them in.

"I can't wait to kill that guy," said Neth.

5

FELLOWSHIP OF FOOLS

Dergar roused Neth and Hops at the crack of dawn ("I didn't even know there was a seven o'clock in the *morning*," grumbled Neth) and within the hour they were astride two horses provided by the king and leading three more, all heavily laden with weapons and equipment. "Every epic journey begins with a single step!" Dergar enthused as they rode out of town. If it weren't for the heavy police presence, Neth would have run him through right then and there. They traveled in silence for almost an hour, and then Dergar pulled up at a lonely tavern well outside the city limits. A weathered wooden sign hanging next to the door identified it as the "Bar None". A second sign, in the window, said "No elfs".

"It's noon somewhere, right?" said Hops.

"We're meeting the rest of our party here!" explained Dergar. He waited for Neth to dismount first, then followed suit, secured the horses, and escorted him inside.

The place was nearly deserted. The proprietor sat behind the bar, arms crossed, in a half-doze. A bard perched on a stool was unenthusiastically playing the latest hit song, "Otto's Irresistible Dance (Resistible Radio Version)", on a lute. The only customers were two dwarfs and an elderly bald man wearing a brown, hooded robe, sharing a table in the far corner. The taller of the dwarfs had positioned himself so that he could see the door, and nodded when Dergar entered. "Neth the Swordsman, meet Yeth, Noe, and Brother Thelonious!" Dergar exclaimed. "Our party is now complete!" Neth frowned. He had nothing against dwarfs – unlike elfs, at least they could hold down a job – but Yeth, the "tall" one, was a walking cliché with his horned helmet, his oversized battle axe, and his outrageous beard/mustache combo that hung well past his junk. Neth hated him instantly. Noe, in contrast, was clean-shaven and dressed rather smartly, like he had a court date. From the looks of him, it would involve something distinctly white-collar – say, investment fraud – that he would inevitably squirm his way out of. In truth, Neth had never seen a clean-shaven dwarf before. It was a little off-putting. The cleric, fidgety and nervous, had dilated pupils and was clearly on something. Probably dryad dust. Neth sighed. As epic quests went, this was looking to be a long one.

"I see you brought lunch!" Yeth said, indicating Hops, who was nervously peeping out of his bag.

"No outside food," said the proprietor, without opening his eyes.

"I'm not lunch," said Hops. "I'm your goddamned *partner!*"

"And fresh, too!" Yeth laughed.

"He's not lunch," Neth repeated. "He's my pet."

"Partner!" insisted Hops.

"Sidekick?" tried Neth.

"A rabbit? Part of our fellowship? Absurd!" cried Yeth.

"Service animals only," droned the proprietor.

"I bite!" hissed Hops.

"As do I," said Yeth, standing up.

"Are we supposed to be intimidated?" Neth asked. "Because you're the same height standing up as you were sitting down."

"Say it again!" barked Yeth, taking up his battle axe.

"Gentlemen, please!" Dergar interjected. "Save your anger for the witch!"

"What's the deal, anyway?" Neth snapped, turning on Dergar. "I thought *I* was the king's big champion? The only one who could kill the witch?"

"*Your* job is to kill the witch!" Dergar said. "*Our* job is to get you to her!"

"I'm not so sure this group is up to the challenge..."

"Bah!" said Yeth. "We have three warriors, an unparalleled strategist..." Noe nodded at this "...and a cleric to heal our wounds and repel the undead. What more do we need?!"

"And a rabbit!" added Hops.

"I agree!" said Dergar. "'Tis a fine party! Strength, vigilance, wisdom, and even luck will not be wanting!"

When they got outside, their horses had been stolen.

"It was elfs," declared Brother Thelonious, shaking his head. "As sure as I'm standing here." He was rubbing something on his gums. "Filthy animals..."

"Garerrit, Palarrin, and Splanderdash!" swore Dergar, casting one of his gauntlets to the ground. Garerrit, Palarrin, and Splanderdash were the three major gods of the region, and saying their names in rapid succession was considered a rather formidable oath. It was also one hell of a mouthful, so most

people stuck with the zingier "Farkas!" It has been suggested that the gods chose their rather cumbersome names for this very reason.

"What's done cannot be undone," Yeth said sagely. Neth resisted the urge to kick him. "We are honor-bound to continue as best we can."

"Wait a minute," said Neth, "we're just going to go on like *this?* On *foot?* We don't even have any equipment!"

"We have weapons, and arms to swing them!" declared Yeth, brandishing his axe.

"What about rations?"

"We'll kill what we eat and eat what we kill!"

"Water?"

"If pressed, we can drink the blood of our enemies!"

"A copy of the *Wilderness Survival Guide*?"

"We don't need that superfluous, pedantic money-grab! We are dwarves, and men!"

"And rabbits!"

"It seems a *rather* long way to walk, at that..." said Noe, nervously twiddling his fingers. Neth decided to put the screws to Dergar.

"You're the King's third ball, Derg. Why don't you mosey back to town and requisition us some fresh gear?" He hooked a thumb at Bar None. "We'll wait for you inside."

"And make sure you requisition an extra handful of silver to cover our bar tab," added Brother Thelonious.

"Brother Thelonious, you are the mouthpiece of the gods!" Dergar cried. "Alcohol is forbidden to you! So say the Sacred Scrolls!" Brother Thelonious shrugged.

"The Sacred Scrolls are open to many

interpretations, my son."

Dergar's shoulders slumped. He hung his head.

"It doesn't matter anyway," he said quietly. "We cannot replace our equipment."

"Why not?" asked Neth.

"It just isn't in the budget," Dergar sighed.

"We're trying to save the kingdom and we have to stay *under budget?*"

"What can we do? The loss of our dragons has crippled us financially. The King has already reduced spending to the bare minimum. He no longer takes his mid-summer holiday, and, last fiscal quarter, **wELFare** – our elf assistance program – was eliminated entirely."

"The subsequent elf riots were a sight to see," said Brother Thelonious. "Fortunately, they only burned down their own part of the forest."

"Gods be damned, this is ridiculous!" protested Neth. "How are we supposed to cross Death Mountain and Death Swamp and Death Estates and the Hills of Death and all those other terrible-sounding places you told me about without horses or supplies?"

"It will take time," said Yeth, "but it can be done."

"Yes!" said Dergar, regaining his enthusiasm. "Doom Mountain presents the only insurmountable obstacle for travelers on foot, and freed from the burden of mounts we can journey *beneath* it!"

"So now our horses were a *burden?*" frowned Neth.

"He's a glass-is-half-full kind of guy," whispered Hops.

"You see," explained Yeth to those who cared, which was nobody, "beneath Doom Mountain there exists an endless labyrinth of interconnected caverns and catacombs, filled with fiendish traps and horrors unimaginable."

"Colloquially, it's known as the Tomb of Utter Bullshit," added Brother Thelonious.

"Amazing," said Neth. "That sounds exactly like a place I don't want to be." Yeth waved a hand dismissively.

"The dangerous passages were sealed off long ago. Now it is simply a single tunnel that burrows straight through the mountain."

"Really, it's safe as houses," added Noe. "There's a toll and everything."

"I like tunnels," said Hops.

"Then it's settled!" said Dergar, holding his sword aloft for emphasis. "On to the Tomb of Utter Bullshit!"

In his extensive mental record of things that suck, Neth decided to move this emprise to the top of the list.

6

THE ROAD TO DOOM MOUNTAIN

In truth, the road to Doom Mountain was an easy one, winding leisurely through farmland and small, quaint towns that the irrepressible hoards of adventurers hadn't discovered yet. (Over the years, Neth had noticed that they always seemed to appear, and congregate, in the same places.) But if Dergar had seemed all business to Neth, Yeth was all business with a business degree, and a minor in more business. Grim and humorless, he marched them a full eighteen hours each day, as if he were out to beat some sort of personal record for "getting to Mount Doom". His brother Noe, on the other hand, was open and friendly, if a bit fey for his kind. In fact, Neth was beginning to suspect that this dwarf had more than a little fairy in his lineage, so to speak. Brother Thelonious, a former adventurer himself, was full of wild stories, and was entertaining the party – well, Noe and Hops, at least – with one now. Frankly, Neth was trying his best *not* to get to know these jokers – they'd be ditching them soon enough. But Hops seemed excited to have new people to talk to.

"What's the most convoluted booby trap you ever had to deal with?" Hops was asking the old cleric. This followed discussions about the scariest monster, weirdest quest, and most fantastic treasure the retired adventurer had ever encountered.

"'Adventurer flambé', we called it," the old man said without hesitation. "We opened a door and a spring-loaded javelin shot out, impaled a guy, and stuck him right to the far wall. Then oil oozed out of several holes in the shaft, a spark was triggered in the spearhead, and the fool went up like a Saturnalia tree left too close to the fire. It didn't cause him as much damage as you'd think, but I'll tell ya, it was a helluva morale killer." He sighed wistfully. "That was back when I was adventuring with the Johannes brothers and that cute little pixie who wore her hair in a human cut. Oh, did they fight over her! Literally, I mean: they had a sword fight over her and killed each other. She ended up marrying a bugbear, as I recall; he came from money. It ended badly but we had some good times along the way. Called ourselves 'The Enchanted Blade Brigade'".

"We should have a name for *our* fellowship!" suggested Noe.

"No, we shouldn't," mumbled Neth.

"A fine suggestion!" said Dergar. "The Fellowship of the... thing. But what thing?"

"The Fellowship of the Rabbit!" said Hops.

"The T Party," offered Brother Thelonious. "The T is for 'Thelonious'."

"The Nuts of the Round Table!" Noe proposed.

"The Knight Shift!" countered Dergar.

"Cleric and the Dominos!"

"The Knights Who Say 'More Butter!'"

"The Adventure People!"

"Band of Brothers!"

"Team Venture!"

"Sparkle Motion!"

"Slaughter and the Blink Dogs!"
"All the Young Druids!"
"Gelatinous, Cubed!"
"Huey Lewis and the News!"

Brother Thelonious knew several old bards' songs (most of them rather racist), and he began to sing one now:

*"Once upon a time
There was a man named Xiqb,
But nothing rhymes with 'Xiqb'
So his story ends here!"*

Hops, Noe, and Dergar laughed and began to sing along. For Neth's money, they couldn't reach the horrors of Doom Mountain soon enough.

7

THE TOMB OF UTTER BULLSHIT

Noe had been right – there *was* a toll to use the foot tunnel beneath Doom Mountain. There was an actual toll booth and everything. There was also a gift shop, a row of vending machines ("Silver Pieces Only"), several portable toilets (Brother Thelonious made for one of these immediately), and an information booth stuffed with brochures promoting travel destinations both near and far: Barovia, Dunwin, Nuthanger Farm, the Desert of Desolation ("Now 20% Less Desolate!"), Ratleaf Forest, Mongo City, the Garden of Zinn, the Yellow Castle ("Now Under New Management!"), and many more. Dozens of tourists, mostly families, were milling about. Everyone in the party was exhausted and hungry, aside from Hops, who'd been carried most of the way and had been able to eat his fill of grass and clover whenever they took a break. In fact, as soon as Neth set him down to stretch his legs Hops began nibbling at an especially attractive patch of grass posted with a "Keep off the Grass!" sign.

Dergar followed Neth as the latter approached the vending machines. Typically, they were sold out of everything except iron rations and Zero bars. Neth didn't have any silver anyway. "Relax, I'm not going anywhere," he said when he noticed Dergar behind him.

"Just making sure!" huffed the captain of the guard.

"So what's the plan?" asked Neth as Yeth and Noe joined them.

"Double-time through the tunnel, and then we rest on the other side!" Yeth said incredulously, as if the very act of asking was ludicrous in the extreme.

"A good plan," nodded Dergar. "Once we're on the other side of the mountain, our journey truly begins."

"I assume you'll be covering our toll," asked Brother Thelonious, returning from the bathroom. He seemed to have a lot more energy now. "It's one gold piece each, you know, and I, of course, have taken a vow of poverty." He folded his hands and bowed his head humbly, but was clearly looking at Dergar out of the corner of one eye.

"And poverty has taken a vow of me," added Neth, returning to the patch of especially tasty grass and scooping up a protesting Hops.

"Er..." said Dergar.

"Er?!" barked Yeth. "What means this 'Er'?"

"It's just that, well, all of our gold was in the saddlebags."

"This gets funnier by the minute," said Hops. "Seriously, we should be filming this."

"Does anyone have ANY money?" cried Yeth, exasperated. Everyone shrugged.

"We could break into one of these snack machines," suggested Brother Thelonious. "How many silver pieces make one gold piece? It's twenty, right?"

"'Tis madness!" said Dergar. "We are on a mission of mercy! Surely if we plead our case the toll collector will see fit to let us pass!"

"This is gonna be good," said Hops, scrunching down in his bag.

The toll collector was a hulking, eight-foot-tall troll, green and rubbery. He wore an undersized cap with "DOT - Dept. of Tunnels" stenciled on it.

"It's a troll booth!" said Noe.

"Yes, that's very droll," sighed the troll. "I've never heard that one before."

Yeth poked Dergar in the ribs with his axe until he stepped forward.

"My good man..." Dergar began. The troll was already frowning. "We are envoys of King Nomolos, on a mission of great urgency. We *must* reach the far side of Doom Mountain, but we were recently beset by rascals and fiends, and our horses and gold were stolen."

"So start climbing," said the troll.

"You fail to appreciate our situation, sir..."

"Look," interrupted the troll. "I see five of you, so that's five gold pieces to use the tunnel. And don't try casting any *invisibility* spells or standing in *single file* to take advantage of my bad eyesight because I know all the tricks."

"Please, Mr. Troll..."

"'Mr. Troll' was my dad's name. My name is Ken."

"Ken..."

"Five gold pieces."

"If you would just..."

"Five. Gold. Pieces."

"...appreciate our dilemma..."

"I don't make the rules, I just follow them."

"Have at thee, then, inflexible, compliant cog!" Yeth suddenly shouted, lunging forward with his

battle axe and neatly splitting the troll in twain from the top of its head to the middle of its chest. Dergar barely got out of the way in time. Yeth pulled his axe free as the two upper halves of the troll sagged to either side, but instead of falling over the troll simply stood there, an annoyed look on its two half-faces.

"Oh, it's on," said the troll as its two halves rapidly grew back together.

"Oh crap!" shouted Neth. "You can't chop up a troll! That's like Monsters 101!"

"In my anger with the system I did forget!" shouted Yeth, bracing himself for battle as the troll tossed its cap aside and barged out the side door of the booth, clenching its fists. Stepping beneath the troll's first, clumsy swing, Yeth swung his axe in a high, wide arc and neatly severed the troll's left arm at the shoulder. He kicked the arm aside. Dergar drew his sword and stepped into the fray. Neth looked around nervously. This was getting serious. A crowd was starting to gather. Noe was frozen with terror. And where was the cleric?

"Neth the Swordsman! We need your sword, man!" shouted Dergar. Neth hesitantly drew his blade. Now seemed like a very good time to run away, but all of these people had seen him. He was a criminal now; he had no choice but to throw in with the group, at least until they got to the other side of the mountain. The troll's severed arm, still imbued with life, had crawled up behind Yeth and grabbed hold of his leg. He struggled to kick it off. Dergar was stabbing the troll again and again, to no avail. Neth gripped his sword with both hands. Maybe if he straight-up decapitated the thing they'd have time to get away before it could...

But before Neth could act Brother Thelonious

reappeared, rushing the troll with a lit torch. As soon as the open flame came in contact with the troll it instantly burst into flame and began to bubble and disintegrate. "Stop, drop, and roll!" yelled a second DOT troll that had just arrived on the scene. But Ken, in a panic, was spinning around and around, peppering friends, enemies, and bystanders alike with flaming chunks of him. The panicked crowd scattered. *"Mommy! Mommy! Is it dying?"* shrieked a small child, tears streaming down her face. Taking advantage of the confusion, someone kicked in the front of the snack machine and stole all the Zero bars.

"Help! Help!" screamed Ken.

"Someone call the authorities!" cried the second troll.

"Quick, into the tunnel!" shouted Brother Thelonious.

Neth and his companions raced into the tunnel beneath Doom Mountain, and didn't stop running until they'd put several miles between themselves and the entrance.

"It smells like pee in here," said Hops when they finally stopped to take a break. He was right, but the tunnel was wide enough to walk two abreast and well-lit by regularly placed torches, so Neth concluded that they didn't have much to complain about. After a few minutes they continued on, walking in silence, each lost in his own thoughts. Dergar was uncharacteristically nervous, constantly looking at the ceiling as if he could feel the millions of tons of mountain above, pressing down on them. Neth, a veteran dungeon crawler, felt right at home. The dwarves and Hops were practically in their element. Brother Thelonious hummed tunelessly and kept his thoughts to himself. In time, calling upon his innate dwarven knowledge of mountains and tunnel work, or possibly his innate ability to bullshit, Yeth announced that they had passed the halfway point.

"Something's wrong," Noe said.

"How do you figure?" asked Brother Thelonious. "This is a DOT tunnel, not a den of monsters. Safe as houses. You said so yourself."

"Yes..." Noe hesitated. "That's just it. This is a very popular thoroughfare. How come we're the only ones using it?"

"They probably closed the tunnel behind us to investigate all the ruckus we caused," Neth sniped, glaring sideways at Yeth. Yeth pointedly ignored him.

"Maybe," Noe agreed. He hesitated again. "But then... why haven't we met anyone coming from the other direction?"

The party froze.

"Er, there could be a lot of reasons, probably," Yeth finally grumbled.

"Maybe they sent ahead word of our little fracas and the cops are waiting for us at the other end," Neth said, glaring at Yeth.

"Impossible!" declared Yeth. "If there were an easy way to get messages over the mountain, this tunnel wouldn't even be necessary!"

"There could be... magical ways..." Brother Thelonious ventured.

"Maybe the troll booth operators on either end of the tunnel use ESP to communicate with one another," Noe suggested.

"Or Banana-Talkies!" chimed in Hops.

"Or passenger pigeons," added Dergar.

"You mean *carrier* pigeons," said Neth. "Passenger pigeons are extinct."

"Oh, not anymore," declared Dergar

"Enough!" Yeth barked. "This is getting us nowhere! We clearly cannot go back so our only choice is to continue forward. Whatever awaits us at the other end of the tunnel, we'll face it when we get there!"

"Four to twenty for assault and battery is what probably faces us at the other end of the tunnel," grumbled Neth as they began walking again.

Fifteen minutes later, they saw it.

About thirty yards ahead, a large, smooth, circular boulder with a spiral carved into one side was blocking the passageway. The party froze. "Farkas!" said Dergar. "Who put that there?"

"Do you think we can climb over it?" asked Yeth, craning his neck to get a better look at the thing. Only now did Neth realize that they had, as one, come to a complete stop. It was as if every one of them could sense that something wasn't right here.

"Maybe they're trying to barricade us in?" asked Dergar.

The boulder moved.

"Oh oh..." said Neth, drawing his sword.

"What, what?" demanded Dergar.

A thick, glistening, organic tube, adorned with several mace-like protuberances, suddenly emerged from the front of the "boulder". The protuberances wavered in their direction.

"Gods, it's a gigantic mollusk!" gasped Dergar. "But what are those things on its head?"

"I've heard of this thing," said Neth.

"Okay, it's absurd enough that it even exists, but you've actually *heard* of it?" asked Hops. Neth ransacked his memory.

"I think it's called a... fail snail?"

"Apt," said the rabbit.

The humongous snail began to move towards them, the mace-like protuberances on its head lashing the air before it. Planting himself in the middle of the tunnel, Neth held his sword at the ready. Now, finally, he was going to get to kill something. He narrowed his eyes and grinned.

The snail was certainly taking a long time to get to him.

Neth impatiently shifted his weight to his other foot. The snail's slow-motion charge was really draining any potential drama from this confrontation.

"Did you know that a snail's teeth are located on its tongue?" Hops offered while they waited. "It has thousands of them, so it uses its long, flat tongue like a file, slowly ripping its meal to pieces."

Neth swallowed nervously. He stopped grinning.

"Maybe," he said, taking a step back, "discretion would be the better part of valor. At least today."

"We can't retreat!" said Yeth, retreating. "They'll arrest us the second we emerge from the tunnel!"

"Does anyone have any salt?" suggested Brother Thelonious.

The entire party was in a slow retreat now, the huge snail advancing on them at a, well, its pace.

"We can't go forward, and we can't go back! What are we going to do?!?" demanded Dergar in a voice that was just a little too high-pitched. He was on the verge of panic. Neth recognized the signs: claustrophobia. The poor man probably felt like the entire tunnel was closing in around him.

"I just hope all the flailing about that monster's doing doesn't bring the roof down on us," Neth said. Dergar groaned dismally.

"You're horrible," whispered Hops.

"The catacombs!" Yeth suddenly exclaimed. "If we cut through the catacombs we can circumvent this part of the tunnel and avoid the beast entirely!"

"You mean the Tomb of Utter Bullshit? I thought you said it was sealed off?"

"It was! But surely there is *some* access, some passage or vent the workmen missed! We only must needs find it!"

"'Must needs find it'?" questioned Hops.

"Noe!" Yeth barked. "Take the left wall of the passage and search for secret doors, concealed doors, hidden doors, false doors, and trap doors! I shall take the right!"

Neth expected the two dwarves to probe the walls with their hands, carefully testing every little crack or blemish. But no, they simply eyeballed each section of wall for a moment and then, shaking their heads, moved on to the next. The snail continued to follow them, and this slow motion retreat/chase continued for some time until suddenly Noe said "Ah ha!" He pressed on a portion of the tunnel wall that looked no different from any other portion of the tunnel wall and a camouflaged earth door on ancient, rusty hinges swung reluctantly inward, expelling a cloud of age-old dust. "Voila!" he said.

"Well done, Brother!" beamed Yeth. "Quickly, everyone, inside!"

Neth looked back at the giant snail, still thirty yards away.

"Or slowly, whichever," he said.

The party did find its way back to the main tunnel, eventually, leaving the offending mollusk far behind, but the process was a total nightmare. The Tomb of Utter Bullshit was a series of interconnected crypts, natural caverns, and hewn stone chambers that followed no logical progression whatsoever. Worse, it seemed that every other room was inhabited by something ridiculous and horrible. In one, the ceiling was actually some sort of predator, superficially resembling a manta ray, that ambushed them, enfolding Noe entirely so that they were forced to kill the thing in order to cut him free. Later, the same thing happened again, only this time it was a false floor that tried to eat them. True to the established pattern, a *wall* attacked the party shortly thereafter, lashing out with jelly-like pseudopods that stunned anyone they touched. The stalactites in one natural cavern they passed through were actually living things that dropped from the ceiling with the clear intent of impaling anyone walking beneath them, and in another cavern several large boulders, also alive, attempted to bowl the party over and crush them to death. Neth was actually relieved when the floating eye monster appeared and simply openly attacked them, until he stabbed it and it immediately exploded, dousing them with poisonous gas. Because it wasn't an eye monster after all: it was a perfectly harmless creature that just happened to look exactly like an eye monster, but was as fragile as a child's balloon. And filled with poisonous gas.

All told, it was, indeed, utter bullshit.

8

THE SWAMP OF THE UNDEAD

There was no toll station at the other end of the tunnel.

"And we actually have money this time," said Neth, counting the handful of coins he'd purloined from the skeletons of the many, many dead adventurers moldering in the Tomb of Utter Bullshit. "Even if it is only ten gold pieces."

"Hey," admonished Brother Thelonious, "when I was your age, ten gold pieces was a lot of money."

"So how far is it to the next point of interest on this joyride?" Neth asked Dergar. "The Swamp of Lingering Death or whatever?"

"The Swamp of the Undead," Yeth corrected him. He pointed his axe roughly southeast, but at the ground. What Neth had initially taken for a barren plain was in fact a bog, which stretched in every direction, as far as the eye could see. "And for all intents and purposes, we are already there."

The only road through the bog snaked north, so of course the party's path led them south. The going was slow and unpleasant. The long, wide, stiff grasses that grew here gave anyone who brushed against them the equivalent of a paper cut, and with each step their feet sunk several inches into the thick mud and had to be pulled free.

"So why is this place called the Swamp of the Undead?" asked Noe.

"Because you can't print 'Shithole Swamp' on a tourist brochure," grumbled Neth.

"Long ago," said Brother Thelonious, "this was the site of a great battle, so great that the dead numbered in the tens of thousands. Many, many of these souls, cut down in the prime of life, were angry... restless... Infused with the lingering dark magicks used by sorcerers on both sides of the battle – magicks so powerful that they had saturated the soil itself – vast numbers of these lost warriors rose again to roam the abandoned battlefield as animated, undying corpses. Still others, their bodies too damaged to rise, returned as spirits, twisted and hateful. So great were their numbers that other, similar beings were drawn to the negative energy they radiated, and soon this entire region was inundated with similar beings."

"So it's the world's number one tourist destination for vampires and spooks," said Neth. "Great."

"Vampires, ghosts, zombies, wights, wraiths... Any creature the grave cannot hold is inevitably drawn to this place..." Brother Thelonious nodded.

"It's why Brother Thelonious was recruited for this quest," Dergar said. "As a cleric, he has the ability to dispel such creatures by drawing on the holy power of his goddess."

"And to heal our injuries," said Brother Thelonious, nodding again. "Under the proper circumstances I can even raise the recently deceased back to life, although this is difficult, and my patron deity will not always grant the request."

"Frith preserve us!" said Hops.

"I'm an agnostic," muttered Neth.

The mud got less and less viscous as they proceeded, the number of trees rising from the moist landscape increased, and by sunset they were in the swamp proper, wading through water that reached Neth's thighs and the middle of the dwarves' chests. They started at the first few plops and splashes they heard as the sky began to darken, certain that something horrible was trying to outflank them, only to realize that the sound came from tiny, electric-blue swamp frogs, leaping from their various hidey-holes into the water.

"They're pretty," smiled Noe.

"They're poisonous," said Yeth.

"It's getting dark. Is it much further?" asked Hops. Riding in Neth's shoulder bag, he was the only one who wasn't soaked to the bone, although the clouds of mosquitoes that had emerged at dusk had taken a particular liking to him so he was no less miserable.

Yeth stopped, so unexpectedly that Dergar ran right into him.

"Yes," the dwarf nodded. "It would be best if we found some high ground and settled in for the night. If we rest until dawn and then set out immediately, we should be through of this horrid place afore the sun sets again."

"But where to find a patch of dry ground large enough to set up camp?" Brother Thelonious asked.

"Maybe that guy knows," Hops said.

"What 'guy'?" snapped Neth.

"Over there, behind those trees," said the rabbit.

They all turned at once.

Facing them from behind a pair of narrow trees was a grey, moldy, humanoid figure clad in armor so old that only the rust was holding it together. For several seconds no one moved, or even dared to breathe. Slowly, Neth drew his longsword from its scabbard, and Dergar, in response, drew his as well. A large centipede scurried out of one of the figure's empty eye sockets and skittered across its scalp.

"Nice touch," whispered Hops.

The thing took a clumsy step towards them.

"It's a zombie!" gasped Dergar.

"I know it's a farking zombie!" hissed Neth.

"Can you dispel it?" Yeth asked Brother Thelonious.

"Yes, but 'twould be better, and easier, to dispatch it with our swords. It would be a grave insult to my goddess to call upon her to turn a single zombie. No pun intended."

"There's two of them," squeaked Hops.

Indeed, another zombie had appeared behind the first. Both were now clumsily closing in.

"Three, four," added Noe. "From the other direction."

"Five, six, a dozen..." said Neth. The animated corpses were rising from the brackish water all around them now. "At what point does your goddess get over herself?"

"Very well!" declared the cleric. "Stand back!"

Since they were surrounded, and there was nowhere to "stand back" to, everyone ducked instead. Brother Thelonious raised his hands over his head and began to chant quietly to himself in a language Neth didn't understand. In short order though he began repeating the same phrase over and over, louder and louder:

"Metton sihn keera, grabes sobor tesh!

"Metton sihn keera, grabes sobor tesh!

"Metton sihn keera, grabes sobor tesh!"

The cleric's hands were glowing now, with a light so pure and bright that Neth and the others had to look away. And then, as if it had always been there, there was a hole in the air, a hole that drew the dozens of zombies surrounding them inside and then vanished as if it had never existed. Brother Thelonious, spent, collapsed into the water. Neth and Dergar quickly helped him up.

"Amazing!" said Dergar. "Never before have I seen such a display of divine power!"

"But where did the zombies go?" asked Noe.

"Working through me, my patron goddess has shunted them into a hastily erected pocket dimension," Brother Thelonious explained.

"But *where*?" Noe pressed.

"What difference does it make?" the cleric gasped, waving a hand dismissively.

"Er, Brother Thelonious, could you do that again?" asked Hops.

"Yes," whispered the cleric, "but not for some time."

"Then I think we're in trouble."

Dismayed, they watched as another score of zombies emerged from the muck.

9

MORE FUN IN THE SWAMP
OF THE UNDEAD

Neth sensed rather than heard something *thwipping* through the air, once, twice, three times in rapid succession. Three of the zombies went down, so quickly that it took him a moment to realize that each one now had an arrow shaft protruding from its noggin. Three more instantly fell in a like manner, and when he turned in the direction the arrows were apparently coming from he spied...

A vision.

Tall, lithe, clad in a forest green ensemble that made her look like a female Robin Hood. She wore her strawberry blonde hair out of the way, in a short bob cut, and her eyes were so blue that they seemed to sparkle. There was a single smudge of dirt on her left cheek, so perfectly placed that it seemed intentional. She was continuing to notch and fire arrows, so rapidly that Neth's eyes couldn't hope to follow. And then she stopped, and smiled as if at some private joke. Every single zombie had been felled. The entire party was staring at her now.

"Uh," said Neth.

"Er," said Brother Thelonious.

"Greetings, travelers," she addressed them. "I am

known as Taelor the Swift."

"I can see that," said Neth, staring in awe.

"My eyes are up here," said Taelor.

It felt so good to have solid ground beneath them that Neth almost didn't mind the dozen or so leeches he subsequently discovered on his legs, or the fact that he appeared to be contracting ringworm.

"So you're a... ranger?" Hops asked Taelor, who had led them here. She knew the swamp like the back of her surprisingly delicate hand.

"Of a sort, talking bunny," she smiled. "I am duty-bound to preserve the natural order of this region, while still protecting those who travel through her."

"There is little 'natural' about the Swamp of the Undead," mumbled Yeth.

"*Wetlands* of the Undead," Taelor corrected him. She stood. "Darkness encroaches and I must be off, but you will be safe and dry here tonight. At dawn I shall return and guide you the remainder of the way."

"Thank you," said Brother Thelonious, standing. Taelor smiled, appreciating the gesture.

"It is my duty," she repeated. "But it is an honor to assist a true gentleman such as yourself."

Brother Thelonious gave her a slight bow.

"And your friends," she added hastily, before departing.

"Hippie," mumbled Yeth as soon as Taelor was out of earshot.

"Yes, but if I were ten years younger..." said Brother Thelonious, staring at her pert little ass as she disappeared into the darkness.

"Not even if you were *thirty* years younger, old man," scoffed the dwarf.

"She's obviously up to no good," said Neth, upending one of his boots to empty the water from it. Something with far more legs than necessary fell out of the boot and quickly scurried off.

"What makes you say that?" asked Noe.

"Have you ever, and I mean *ever*, encountered a beautiful woman in the course of a quest who wasn't a plant or a traitor or some sort of monster in disguise? Best case scenario – and I mean the *best* – she swipes all your equipment as soon as you fall asleep, after giving you the clap."

"Well, I've, er..." Noe took a deep breath and clearly made a decision. "I've never been on a quest before," he declared boldly.

"Seriously?" asked Neth.

"Enough of this!" snapped Yeth. "Noe, collect wood for a fire! I shall take the first watch! We march at dawn!"

That night, Neth had the strangest dream.

He was curled up with Taelor, who was cooing in his ear and nuzzling his neck, when, regrettably, nature's call compelled him to disentangle himself from the lovely young ranger and rise. As he urinated against a tree several yards from their camp, he looked back and realized – in that hazy, disconnected manner one often adopts in dreams – that everyone else was asleep. No one was on guard duty. The fire was almost out, but the glow of the dying embers cast just enough light for him to watch the white, pig bladder balloon that bobbed about the camp. A child must have lost it. He watched as the balloon visited each of his companions in turn. Except Hops, he realized. That made him sad. Hops put on a lot of airs, but Neth knew he would've enjoyed playing with the balloon. If he'd been awake, of course. After a time the balloon flew away, up, up into the night sky. "Bye bye, balloon!" he said, waving. "Bye bye!" He went back to bed.

As promised, Taelor returned at dawn, and while the path she led them on meandered considerably and even, Neth could have sworn, doubled back on itself a couple of times, at least they didn't encounter any more undead monstrosities. The girl knew what she was doing. That's not to say the going was entirely pleasant, however. Excluding Hops, everyone was bone tired, as if they hadn't slept a wink. Worse, they were covered with animal bites – something had gotten to them in the night. "I hope it wasn't anything poisonous..." worried Dergar.

"We'll find out when we start dropping dead," snapped Neth. He was irritable, they were all irritable. When Hops made a witty observation equating the words *undead* and *inflammable*, no one humored him. Neth just told him to shut up.

The second night fell, and they were still in the Wetlands of the Undead.

"The safest route is not necessarily the most direct route!" Taelor snapped when Yeth confronted her. They had set up camp in another dry clearing, remarkably similar to the first.

"Woman, if you are toying with us..." growled Yeth.

"You will be free of the wetlands by midday tomorrow. And I, thankfully, will be free of you!" She stalked off. "On the morn, then!" she shouted without looking back.

"Something's not right here," said Yeth.

"For once, I agree with you, short stack," said

Neth. Hops was sniffing the air.

"This is the same place we stayed last night, I'm sure of it," Hops said.

"That clinches it," said Neth, scooping the rabbit up. "Hops and I are going to follow her!"

"You're going to run out on us, you mean!" said Dergar, brandishing his sword and blocking Neth's path. "You're not going anywhere!"

"She's going to get away, you stupid flumph!" said Neth, dropping Hops and drawing his longsword.

"*What* did you call me?" snarled Dergar.

"Stop, both of you!" said Brother Thelonious. "The rabbit can stay here and I will accompany the swordsman in pursuit of our mysterious benefactor!" Dergar relaxed.

"Very well," he grumbled, sheathing his blade.

Neth and the cleric set off after Taelor, who was already nearly out of sight.

10

HEAD GAMES

Moving as stealthily as possible, Neth and Brother Thelonious tailed the comely ranger for several miles, and it was the wee hours of the morning by the time she reached the dilapidated cabin that was apparently her home, or at least her current base of operations. Slowly, carefully, the two men crept up to the ramshackle structure. Neth wrinkled his nose.

"Do you smell that?" he whispered.

"The smell of evil," Brother Thelonious said solemnly. Neth rolled his eyes.

"It's meat, or a butchered animal or something."

"It could be evil," insisted the cleric. "Evil smells like that sometimes."

Neth shushed him; they were right at the front door now. Sliding a loose board aside, Neth peeped inside. The ranger, partially illuminated by the moonlight that shone through a large hole in the roof, was sitting in a flimsy wooden chair, motionless.

"What's she doing?" asked Brother Thelonious. "Is she changing clothes?"

"No!" said Neth. "She's just... sitting there. Sleeping, maybe? I can't see her face."

"It smells like someone gutted a deer in there," Brother Thelonious said. He was rubbing something on the inside of his nose. "Peppermint oil, to mask the smell," he said defensively when Neth frowned at him.

"Okay," said Neth. "I'm going in. Be ready to back me up." The cleric nodded.

Several seconds passed, but Neth didn't move.

"Are you going in tonight?" asked Brother Thelonious.

"I was just trying to think of something cool to say when I barge in there. Something hard-boiled and accusatory, but not so insulting that I ruin my chances with her if we're wrong."

"Have you ever heard the phrase 'the wit of the staircase'?"

"No. What is that?"

"It's when you think of the perfect thing to say, but only *after* the stunningly beautiful ranger has perforated you with a dozen arrows and kicked your dead body down the staircase."

"You're a great comfort, padre," Neth grumbled. Steeling himself, he swung the door open. The figure in the chair didn't move. The interior of the cabin was blue with moonlight, bright enough to see, but the chair sat in the far corner, in the shadows.

"I've come to talk to you," Neth announced dramatically. *Damn,* he thought, *that was pretty weak.*

The figure in the chair didn't respond.

Neth approached the figure slowly, slowly, ready to hit the floor if he even thought he heard an arrow being notched. But nothing happened, and a few seconds later he was looking at the place where Taelor's head used to be.

"By the gods..." he whispered.

"All clear?" said a voice directly behind him. Neth

nearly soiled himself. He *really* had to go to the bathroom, he realized.

"Don't sneak up on people like that!" he whisper-shouted.

"I don't think she can hear us," Brother Thelonious said, indicating Taelor's headless body. "I wonder what got her?" Neth craned his neck to examine the body more closely. His lower lip began to tremble.

"Oh, oh no..." he said, stepping back. "I think I'm gonna be sick..."

"What? What?" asked Brother Thelonious. Neth spoke slowly and haltingly.

"Whatever... got her... it... it scooped out... all her innards..." That was it – putting it into words was too much for him. He started to retch.

"No!" shouted Brother Thelonious, slapping his hand over Neth's mouth, holding the sick in. Neth's cheeks bulged. "Don't vomit, you fool! The evil in this place is almost palpable! We mustn't leave any signs that we've been here!" Neth gestured helplessly. He was already vomiting, or he would be, as soon as Brother Thelonious got his hand out of the way.

"Mmmphm!" he said.

"Swallow it!" demanded Brother Thelonious. Neth shook his head back and forth.

"Swallow it!"

Neth swallowed it.

"I didn't even think... it was possible... to swallow it..." Neth gasped as they stumbled outside.

Brother Thelonious froze.

"What?" said Neth. Then he felt it too. A rippling in the air; a dank, organic stench that, somehow, he seemed to *hear* rather than smell. His head began to pound, as if a cold, wet hand had reached through his skull and was squeezing his brain. Head reeling, Neth shoved brother Thelonious into a concealing patch of foliage and dove in next to him. A moment later they saw it: a vague shape against the full moon, dark but trailing tiny, twinkling, dull-green lights, as if it were attended by sickly fireflies. It dove out of the sky and circled the cabin, once, twice, three times, before finally entering through the hole in the roof. "What *is* that?" whispered Neth. The cleric shrugged. Keeping low, the two men carefully circled to the west side of the hovel and approached the broken window they found there. The jagged glass still in its frame reflected the moonlight like silver teeth. Slowly, they peered in over the sill.

The ranger sat in the rickety chair, head restored, apparently none the worse for wear. Her eyes sparkled and she wore a thin, knowing smile, one that was directed inward, as if at some private joke. Absently, she wiped a trickle of blood from the corner of her ruby red lips with a single finger. She sighed contentedly, as one sated. Then, closing her eyes, she arched her back and slowly ran her hands up and down her body, as if reveling in the tactile reality of it. *She is so beautiful...* Neth found himself thinking. *So beautiful...*

Taelor snapped to attention, startling the two men outside. She began laughing, a hysterical laugh that deteriorated into a joyous scream, and now she was whipping her head back and forth, back and forth, faster and faster, and before Neth and Brother Thelonious' horrified eyes a bloody gash opened at the base of her neck and her head *separated from her body,* rising, under its own power, into the air.

But that wasn't the worst of it.

The worst of it was that her internal organs – heart, lungs, intestines, all of it – were still attached to the flying head, dangling beneath it like the ornaments on a deranged butcher's holiday tree. Pale green lights flickered from deep within the vitals, reinforcing the simile. Neth felt his gorge rising again.

"Why, why, why, does that even *exist?*" he lamented. "Why is it even a *thing?*"

"Meh, I'd still hit it," shrugged Brother Thelonious.

The airborne monstrosity swooped around the room, gibbering incoherently to itself, as if it were speaking in tongues – which made the whole scenario even more disturbing, somehow – and then it hurdled through the hole in the roof and disappeared into the night.

"I know what it is we face," Brother Thelonious said solemnly. "It is a... penanggalan."

"A what?"

"A vampire, of sorts. It fed on us last night, and it's been leading us in circles so that it can feed on us again. It's probably 'guiding' several victims through the swamp at any given time. It must be destroyed." Neth nodded, drawing his blade.

"I'll handle this," he said.

"No!" said the cleric. "It's immune to weapons of any type. According to the copper dreadfuls I used to read back at the monastery, a penanggalan can only be destroyed by preventing the head and body from reuniting."

"Copper dreadfuls? Are you telling me that our resident 'expert' gleaned all his knowledge about the undead from trashy horror magazines???"

Brother Thelonious shrugged.

"Okay, so what do the *copper dreadfuls* suggest that we do?" asked Neth, throwing his arms up in exasperation.

"Clearly she can walk around in daylight in her

human form, but platinums to parsley the head is fully susceptible to sunlight when separated from the body."

"'Platinums to parsley'?"

"I just came up with that," Brother Thelonious smiled. "You like it?"

Neth sighed heavily. He was getting a tension headache.

"We must sabotage the body," Brother Thelonious continued, unabashed. "Fill the empty cavity with something unpleasant or toxic so that she can't or won't reassemble. Then, when the sun comes up, she explodes, probably. Or melts. Something appropriately dramatic, I'm sure."

"So... fill her up with lamp oil or something."

"Exactly, except we don't have any lamp oil. You know what would've been perfect? Salt. This is the second time in as many days it would've been useful to have a quantity of salt on hand. I need to remember to bring some along next time. It's the little things, you know? I was once acquainted with this fellow who always carried a lump of clay, just an ordinary lump of clay, but that came in handy more times than..."

"Would you focus, please?" shouted Neth.

"I told you what we need to do!" Brother Thelonious shouted back. *"Sabotage the body!"*

"We don't have anything to sabotage the body *with!* If I may quote myself at age thirteen, I say we just set it on fire and see what happens, because we really need to wrap this up. I'm cold, I'm tired, and I really have to go to the bathroom..." He trailed off. He'd had an epiphany.

"What are you doing?" asked Brother Thelonious as Neth strode purposefully into the cabin.

"Sabotage," said Neth.

As always, Yeth was the first to wake. He sat up, stretched, cracked his back, and then surveyed the camp. He frowned. No one was on guard duty, again. And where was the reluctant swordsman, and the old man? He briefly wondered if the former had slipped away during the night, perhaps pursued by the latter? But then he saw the rabbit curled up with Noe, both fast asleep, and dismissed the idea. The swordsman wouldn't have cut and run without his furry companion. Then he remembered – they'd gone after the girl. Hadn't they come back yet? The buffoons had probably gotten lost. Well, no choice but to wake the others and begin the search. But first things first.

Relieving himself against a nearby tree, he actually took a moment to appreciate his surroundings. Despite the overall dismalness of this place, it was a beautiful morning. The sun, already well above the horizon, was bright. Birds were singing. A strange, ululating sound was getting closer and closer...

What in...?

It was men, making their way towards the sleeping party. The dwarf picked up his battleaxe and readied himself. He could hear them clearly now, bellowing their fool heads off and tearing hell-bent through the marsh as if the Devil himself were hot on their heels. Why, he wondered briefly, must men always be so histrionic? A few seconds later the swordsman burst from a copse of trees about thirty yards away, running hell-for-leather, followed in short order by the old man. *"Run for your life!"* shrieked the swordsman as they ran right past him. *"Sunlight doesn't affect it and it's mad as hell!!!"*

Yeth stood his ground, and a moment later, when a

flying, gibbering monstrosity hurtled by in pursuit of the two men, he calmly but savagely batted it out of the air with the flat of his axe. Propelled across the clearing, it smashed into the trunk of a tree with a sickening *CRACK* and then slid to the ground, its eyes rolled back in its head. The entire party, awake now, slowly gathered around the thing.

"Ugh, what is it?" Dergar wondered aloud.

"And why does it smell like number two?" asked Noe.

11

THE RELATIVELY PLEASANT HILLS

Using the sun as a guide, the party struck out due east and reached the Relatively Pleasant Hills the following day. The hills were aptly named, and nothing deleterious happened there.

12

PLAIN AWFUL

Too soon the hills fell behind them, gradually flattening out into a wide open expanse of caked earth and tenacious, scrubby plant life, almost but not quite a desert. The air, harsh and dry, was unpleasant to breathe. As they marched silently, each lost in his own thoughts, Neth noticed several dots in the far distance, closing in on them. "Incoming at whatever o'clock that is," he said, gesturing in the dots' direction. The party stopped, readied their weapons, waited. There was nowhere to go. They would have to fight. As the dots got closer Neth recognized them as dogs, wild dogs.

And because their world was both ridiculous and horrible, each dog had two heads.

"Why," bemoaned Neth, his shoulders slumping, "do they have two heads? What possible evolutionary advantage...?"

The pack, close now, charged them.

"Argh! It's biting me twice at once!" screamed Dergar as one of the dogs clamped onto him with two sets of jaws. "Help! Help!"

"So is that one for evolution, or one for intelligent design?" asked Hops as Neth gently dropped him to the ground.

"Not now, you nonsensical rodent!" snapped Neth, leaping into the fray.

"I'm not a rodent! I'm a lagomorph!" Hops shouted after him. One of the dogs turned a single head towards the sound. With a frightened squeak, Hops quickly scampered into some nearby brush, escaping only because the dog, each head having selected a different target, tried to run in opposite directions simultaneously and fell flat on its faces.

"Definitely not *intelligent* design," Neth said, running the animal through.

The dog attack was a harbinger of things to come, for the plains proved to be the stage for an endless parade of seemingly random encounters, each more incongruous and preposterous than the last.

While resting inside a lonely, dilapidated house that stood, inexplicably, in the middle of nowhere, they were attacked by the ghost of a unicorn, which Brother Thelonious was able to dispel only with great difficulty. Later, while sleeping upstairs, they learned, much to their dismay, that giant bedbugs are a thing. No one protested when Neth insisted on burning the house down.

They met a caravan of elfs heading in the opposite direction who, naturally, tried to sell them meth. Not long after, Yeth discovered that his wallet was missing.

Humanoid praying mantises wearing yellow robes verbally accosted them from a safe distance and tried to get them to join some mosquito god cult.

Hops was almost swallowed whole by an enormous toad which he had incautiously approached because, as he put it, "We both hop, so I assumed we'd be natural allies."

A gigantic owl carried Noe off one night. The final vote was 3-2 in favor of rescuing him, so a side quest was undertaken to do so. Once located, the owl, which turned out to be far more intelligent (and reasonable) than anyone had anticipated, ultimately sold Noe back to them for three gold pieces.

Giant spiders attacked the party. ("No square-cube law in this universe, I see," observed Hops.) Afterwards, fisticuffs broke out during a heated debate over what constituted a "giant" spider as opposed to a merely "huge" spider.

Mostly, though, it was a long, tortuous, boring slog, characterized by tedium and petty bickering. Days sank into nights bled into days, until they lost all track of time. The journey seemed endless, but, like any miserable experience, eventually it led to something worse.

13

THE CASTLE OF SAND AND ICE

"There. Do you see it?"

Neth squinted.

"I see it," said Hops. Then the others did too. A flash of light; something reflecting the sun from a point just above the horizon.

"Princess Skylark's castle of sand and ice," Dergar whispered reverently.

"Does this castle actually have a name?" asked Neth. "Because 'Princess so-and-so's castle of blah blah blah' is kind of a mouthful." Dergar ignored him.

"We're almost there, lads!" he boomed, increasing his stride. "And then our swordsman can complete his quest!"

"The rest of us don't have to go in, do we?" asked Noe. "I mean, we can just wait outside while he wraps things up, right?"

"Oh, no," said Neth. "Dergar said that your job is to escort me to the sorceress, so you are damn well going to escort me right up to her, right up in her personal space, whether she's holed up in the highest tower of the castle or taking a long, luxurious dump in the privy, got it?"

"So we shall!" declared Dergar. "Just be sure to do *your* job once we get there!"

He's really looking forward to this, Neth thought. *Everyone else is dragging ass, but he's got a grin on his face like a kid on his way to his first nudie show. He really can't wait to watch me lop this broad's head off.*

Slowly, inexorably, the castle came into view. Jutting out of the cracked earth like a glistening stalagmite, its outer walls and towers shone like polished steel, and it did indeed appear to be formed out of dirty ice – the castle proper a single, solid entity, as if it had grown there. Despite the prevailing temperature – warm, but not uncomfortably so – the ground around the castle boasted a thick covering of snow. Someone had even built several snowmen, complete with stick arms, coal eyes, and carrot noses, which stood haphazardly just beyond the front gate, as if guarding the courtyard. Was the princess a child? Neth wasn't too keen on the idea of murdering a child. Not for a lousy five thousand silver pieces.

"I like the looks of those carrots," said Hops.

"Shush," hissed Neth, all business now. Cautiously, he stepped into the courtyard. The gate was wide open, as if they were expected, but aside from the snowmen the courtyard was empty. Up close, he could see the particulate inside the walls, feel the cold emulating from them. It really was a castle formed of ice and sand. Where did people come up with this shit? Slowly, he made his way towards the largest, highest tower, and the others followed. The deep, virgin snow made each step an inelegant chore, and Neth dreaded the idea of engaging in any sort of combat in these conditions. He hesitated. *Which is exactly why we shouldn't have come in here,* he realized.

The portcullis dropped down at that very instant,

sealing off the gated entrance and trapping them inside. "You're trespassing," said a voice above them. Neth looked up. A youngish woman with long, curly, pitch-black hair, wearing a pair of unflattering pajamas, stood on a low balcony, glaring at them. She had a pug nose, smallish breasts, thick legs, and a little bit of heft in the aft, but while these individual attributes were far from remarkable the cumulative effect was nothing less than... gorgeous. "You're trespassing," the woman repeated, rubbing sleep from her eyes, "and it is seven o'clock in the morning. What do you want?" Dergar stepped forward, stumbling in the deep snow, and pointed an accusing finger at her.

"Justice!" he cried. The woman frowned slightly and furrowed her brow.

"He's not here," she finally said.

"She's a comedian," grumbled Yeth. Dergar continued, unabated.

"Princess Skylar Skylark, bane of Nogard, consort of demons and of beasts in the fields, I hereby accuse thee of poaching, of theft, and of general malfeasance! In the name of King Nomolos, surrender to us immediately or face the blade of our champion!" Princess Skylark scrutinized the intruders. Besides the blowhard, there were two midgets, an old man who was openly ogling her, a relatively normal-looking guy, and, peeping out of the normal guy's shoulder bag, a rabbit.

"And which one of you is this... champion?" she asked.

"He is," said Dergar, pointing to Neth.

With a flick of Princess Skylark's wrist, Neth was lifted several feet into the air. Hops, no fan of heights, immediately leapt free and instantly disappeared into the hole his body punched in the deep snow. Neth floated up, up, until he was eye to eye with the witch. She examined him carefully, taking special note of his equipment. "Ah," she smiled, "a Bag of Holding! That will do nicely." With a jerk of her head Neth's magical bag tore itself free and opened of its own accord. "Buh-bye, champion." Neth felt himself being inexorably drawn towards, and then into, the magical bag. First his hand was inside it, then his entire arm. It was impossible! Yes, the space inside the bag was infinite, but there was no way he could fit through the mouth! And yet, somehow, he did. Inch by inch the Bag of Holding consumed him, until he was gone. The bag sailed through the air into Skylar's outstretched, fully reconstituted hand and she neatly tied it shut. "Your champion is defeated," she announced to the rest of the party. "Snow fiends..." she trailed off, before twirling and disappearing into the castle.

"Did she just call us 'snow fiends'?" asked Dergar, in a huff.

"Well, you did accuse her of doing it with animals..." said Noe.

"I think *those* are the snow fiends, my friends," said Brother Thelonious, indicating the snowmen scattered around the courtyard. They were beginning to *move*. Yeth attempted to ready his axe, but the snow was up to his chest, and the best he could do was hold it above his head. The snow fiends glided in, moving through the deep snow like water, as if they were a part of it, or it wasn't even there. Clumsily, Yeth swung his axe and split the closest fiend at the shoulder. Backing off, it used its stick arms to scoop up fresh snow and quickly repair itself. Meanwhile, the fiends farthest from the party were using the same snow to rapidly build new snow fiends.

"They're made of snow!" cried Dergar. "How do

you fight *snow?*"

"Salt!" cried Brother Thelonious, throwing his arms up in exasperation. "Again we could have used the salt!"

"Would you shut up about the salt?" shouted Yeth.

The snow fiends, increasing in number by the minute, closed in.

14

IN THE BAG

Neth slowly opened his eyes. He was dizzy, slightly nauseated, and laying on his back in a bright, steel room, staring at a pair of long, flickering lights hanging from the ceiling. The lights gave off an annoying buzz, and the flickering made his eyes hurt. Carefully, he sat up. The room, medium-sized, was filled with a vast array of *stuff* – weapons, personal belongings, household goods, knick-knacks, treasure – each item meticulously labeled with a yellow tag sporting a multi-digit number. Checking himself for injuries, he found that he too was wearing one of the yellow tags. Apparently, he was #44715-1319211413/OR. He tore the tag off and cast it aside.

Now what? There was a door on the far side of the room, but he wasn't ready to try it just yet. He could hear the bustle of activity beyond, and, occasionally, voices, but he couldn't make out what they were saying, or even the language. But first things first. He'd dropped his longsword when he'd been sucked into the bag. He needed a weapon. He picked up the first sword he saw. Solid, good heft. It would do. But something made him hesitate. Setting the perfectly acceptable blade aside, he began rifling through the items in the room, not sure what he was looking for but accepting the fact that he would recognize it when he found it. And when he did find it, when his hand closed around the hilt, he knew. *This* sword spoke to him. He tore the yellow tag off and claimed it as his own. Now. Now he was ready to go through that door.

The door swung open easily, and he found himself on a solid, steel catwalk, overlooking a room of immense proportions. Rows upon rows of metal shelving dominated this room, the shelves laden with thousands upon thousands of apparently random items, both mundane and bizarre. And there was something – several somethings, actually – zipping about among those rows of shelves, although, from where he stood, he couldn't see who or what they were. The door closed behind him with a click, and as he turned to see if he'd just locked himself out he saw the two-foot-tall goblin rushing down the catwalk towards him. He raised his new sword and readied himself for battle, but the goblin, who was dressed quite neatly (particularly for a goblin) didn't even notice. "Step aside, coming through!" said the creature, ducking past him. It was carrying a heavily scented candle and what, in another time and place, would be referred to as a "marital aid". The goblin disappeared around a corner at the far end of the catwalk. Instinctively, Neth tried the door he had just come through. It wasn't locked, but there was really no reason to go back into the room he'd just come out of. He followed the goblin.

It turned out there were a *lot* of goblins. Hundreds of them, all wearing the same uniform, all dashing purposefully about, most carrying one or more entirely random items. A few glanced at him curiously, but mostly they ignored him. Reaching a metal staircase, Neth descended to the main floor then hesitated, unsure what to do next. *"Boblet Bodaggin to receiving dock L! Boblet Bodaggin to receiving dock L!"* blared a distorted, metallic voice that seemed to come from nowhere and yet everywhere at once. Neth was so startled by the voice that he nearly jumped out of his shorts, but none of the goblins paid any attention to it.

Where the hell *was* he?

Approaching the nearest shelf – while indifferent goblins hurried by, weaving around him – Neth examined its contents more carefully. Just like in the room above, it was an apparently random collection of, well, stuff, although each object was clearly labeled with one of the yellow tags and each tag was, it seemed, individually numbered. The shelves were numbered too, he realized, with bright green tags. Some of the items they held were brand new, but others were well-worn, obviously quite used. A few seemed maddeningly out of place, even here, like the ham sandwich he was currently staring at. On impulse, Neth removed the tag attached to the sandwich and swapped it out for that of a shimmering golden dagger on the shelf just below it.

"Hey, you there! What do you think you're doing?"

"Uh," said Neth, turning around. A goblin dressed marginally more nicely than the others was staring at him, hands on its hips. It was carrying a clipboard and wore a faded necktie with mallard ducks on it.

"Visitors are *not* to touch the entrusted items, ever! They should have made that perfectly clear when you signed in!"

"Okay," Neth said quickly. "Sorry." The goblin wearing the mallard duck necktie continued to stare at him, suspicious.

"Who are you, anyway?" it asked.

"My name's, uh, Dergar," Neth said.

"And who are you here with?" the goblin pressed.

"I think his name was... Rick?" Neth cringed even as he said it.

"Let me see your visitor's badge," the goblin said, stepping towards him. Neth was stymied. He couldn't possibly fight all million-hundred of these little bastards, and subterfuge was clearly not working. There was only one option left. He bolted. *"Get him!"* screamed the goblin in the tie as Neth ran down the nearest aisle. The other goblins ignored him.

"They don't pay me enough to 'get' anyone," one of them mumbled.

15

THE RABBIT STEWS

Hops carefully poked his head out of the snow at a point several feet from where he'd fallen in. He had burrowed here under the surface over the last several minutes. He was good at burrowing, but he generally didn't burrow through snow, and now his front paws were numb and tender to the touch. For the first minute or so that he was digging there had been a lot of racket – fighting, no doubt – but afterward, and quite suddenly, it had grown eerily silent. Hops felt vaguely guilty for not helping the others fight the enchanted snowmen, but he would have contributed little. Better that at least one of them avoid capture. Now, shivering with cold, Hops cautiously examined the courtyard. Everyone, including the snowmen, was gone. Slipping out of his snow tunnel, he scampered for the nearest wall and then hugged it as he made his way to the far end of the courtyard and the large, ornate doors that opened into the castle proper. He wasn't quite sure what he would do when he got there. He couldn't open doors. He briefly considered digging down, under the walls, but the ground was frozen solid this close to the ice castle, and his digging feet already hurt terribly. Besides, there was no way of knowing just how deeply the walls were embedded into the earth. Maybe miles.

Well, he would just have to figure something out. It was up to him now. He hunkered down and made himself as small and compact as possible – as much for warmth as to remain unseen – and took up a position next to the front doors. Maybe, when someone eventually opened them, he could surreptitiously dart inside. It wasn't much of a plan, but it was better than nothing.

16

PURSUED BY THE JOB-GOBLINS

Neth ran, leaping over terrified goblins and sweeping items off the shelves behind him to impede his pursuers. Because now he *was* being chased. *"All security to quadrant T. All security to quadrant T!"* echoed the disembodied, metallic voice. Behind him, a score of goblins in blue uniforms, wielding wands that crackled with electricity, were in hot pursuit, shoving their contemporaries aside in their haste to reach him. After twisting and turning through row after row of metal shelving, Neth finally spied a proper, solid wall ahead of him, at the end of this row. If he followed it, he was certain to come upon a door that led... well, someplace, hopefully. The security goblins were a good way behind him – with his longer legs, he was easily able to outdistance them on the straightaways – but now he was in far more danger of being boxed in, especially if this wall met another one, effectively trapping him in a corner. He had to do something to slow them down. Skidding to a halt, he turned back and threw all of his weight into one of the shelving units that formed the aisle he'd just exited. It was solid enough to wrench his shoulder, but he felt it wobble so he renewed his efforts, pushing with all his might until his face flushed red from the strain. *"No!"*

shrieked one of the pursuing goblins as it realized what Neth was doing, but it was too late. The entire unit toppled over, sending a neatly stacked set of ceramic dishes, a gleaming silver helmet, what appeared to be an ordinary bundle of sticks (fastened with twine), a can of chili, a stuffed jaguar, several stoppered glass flasks filled with a bubbling orange liquid, and sundry other items plummeting into the aisle on top of them. Several of these items broke. *"Oh my God!"* someone wailed. Crashing into the shelf next to it, the falling unit almost took its neighbor out as well, but, after teetering once, the second shelf just barely managed to maintain its vertical integrity. Instead, the compromised shelf slowly slid sideways along the stable shelf's face with an extended metallic screech, hit the wall, and then rapidly fell to the floor with a deafening crash, its base striking a nearby cart laden with various objects marked "FRAGILE" and launching it into a rubbernecking worker goblin, effectively knocking the wind out of him. The worker goblin, dropping to his knees, tried to grab the cart for support but only succeeded in tipping it over, scattering its contents across the floor. There was some sort of alarm going off now, but Neth didn't even notice. The security goblins were already clambering over the fallen shelf. Sprinting full-bore along the wall, he felt confident of his escape now, until a moment later when a dozen more security goblins, their wands sizzling, spilled out of two of the rows in front of him. He attempted to brake so abruptly that the upper half of his body was still moving and he tumbled forward, did a near-perfect somersault, landed on his chest, and then slid several more yards across the preternaturally smooth floor before he actually came to a stop. Behind him, some (though not all, he noted with some satisfaction) of the group that had originally been pursuing him were closing in. The one in the lead was saturated with orange goop, and one of his eyes was already swelling shut from something hitting him in the face. But he smiled with malicious glee, repeatedly triggering his electric wand so that it popped and spat ominously. "Oi, yepper, boyo, Imma gonna shove this 'ere taze-wanner right up yer bumboose, I am!" he said with great satisfaction. "Then, maybe after a' hour or three, we'll start the interrogation proper and find out just who the blork ye are and what the skaff yer doin' here..."

"I don't even know where I am!" Neth cried. "This crazy bitch shoved me into my own Bag of Holding and somehow I ended up here!" The goblins froze, eyes wide. Several jaws hit the floor and they let out a collective gasp. Slowly, they lowered their wands.

"Egadzooks," said their self-appointed spokesman, his voice trembling. "You're a *client?*"

17

THE RABBIT ACTS

Hours passed, and the sun was much higher in the sky when two of the snowmen – snow *fiends*, the witch had called them – opened the front doors from the inside and proceeded to loiter in the open doorway. They didn't even notice Hops, scrunched low and tight against the outside wall. One of the snow fiends held a cigarette in its clumsily formed mouth. Producing a palm-sized, convex lens – a burning glass – the snow fiend expertly focused a beam of sunlight on the end of the cigarette until it began to smolder. "Those things'll melt ya, ya know," grumbled the other fiend, its voice like cracking icicles. The first snow fiend gave the approximation of a shrug.

"Gotta melt from something," it said.

Creeping carefully past them, Hops slipped inside.

The interior of the castle was surprisingly sumptuous, for an edifice made out of dirty ice, at least. The castle had an open, flowing layout with few doors. Expensive carpets and rugs covered most of the floors, at least in highly trafficked areas, the furniture was low-key and tasteful, and even the artwork – paintings, mostly, with an emphasis on landscapes – was stylish and subtle, if somewhat unchallenging. Hops encountered a few snow fiends, but they weren't exactly on the lookout for a rabbit and he easily avoided them. Methodically, he explored each and every room on the ground floor. (There were several sets of stairs leading upwards, but he ignored these. Only usurped boy princes and virgin princesses were imprisoned in towers. Commoners like his friends were thrown in the dungeon.) The rabbit turned up little of interest until he poked his head into the cold(er) storage room behind the kitchen. There, the smell of meat was almost overpowering, and when he ventured inside he discovered hundreds of cuts, all carefully wrapped in butcher paper and fussily bound with twine. Each packet had been neatly hand-labeled, and, apparently, each one contained the same type of meat. "Oh, wow," Hops said to himself as the truth sunk in. "That's... unexpected." Slipping out of the cold storage room he investigated the dry goods pantry next, and he almost did a happy binky bunny dance at what he found there: the Bag of Holding! It had been casually tossed on the floor, alongside several larger bags filled with flour, salt, and the like. But what now? The bag was tied shut, and he couldn't work knots. Still, he had to try something. So he did what rabbits do best. He began to chew.

18

THE FELLOWSHIP CONSUMMATED

"This is, as you might imagine, highly unregular," said the goblin behind the desk. "Highly unregular," he repeated. He was quite nervous. Neth helped himself to another ginger snap. The bowl on the desk was almost empty.

"Yeah, but I got in so there must be a way to get out, right?" Neth pressed.

"Nondubitably, nondubitably," the executive goblin said quickly. "It's just that, well, there are rules and regulations and so on and so forth *et sic porro...*"

"Enlighten me," said Neth, munching on his cookie.

"It's just that, well, only the client – that is, the owner of a bag – may extract entrusted objects from it, you see, and as you are the owner, and you are here..."

"The way I see it," Neth said carefully, "you are looking at one hell of a lawsuit here." The executive goblin blanched.

"Now, now," he said quickly, "I'm sure we can solve this problem without all that legal fiddlebaloo. And, naturally, we'll throw in a few extras to make up for your time and trouble. Extra storage, perhaps?"

"Naturally," said Neth, making a show of

examining the now empty cookie bowl.

"Oh, yes," said the executive goblin quickly. "I'll send for more ginger snaps."

There was some sort of ruckus outside the office. Shouting and running.

"Oh, *now* what?" groaned the goblin, leaping from his chair. "Excuse me, just for a moment, please," he said. Curious, Neth followed him out the door and onto the warehouse floor.

Worker and security goblins alike raced past them in terror, and a light wind was somehow blowing here, inside the building, already sweeping lighter objects towards what everyone was fleeing from: a gigantic, gaping hole in the far wall, through which a monstrously large creature was staring at them. Monstrously large, but kind of cute. And shockingly familiar, Neth realized.

"Hops!" he cried, running towards the gargantuan rabbit. The wind was picking up, its strength increasing exponentially, and suddenly everything that wasn't nailed down or actively resisting was being drawn inexorably towards the huge rend in the wall.

"Oh oh..." said Neth.

Hops bounded out of the kitchen as, accompanied by a dull booming sound, it was almost instantly filled from wall to wall and ceiling to floor with all manner of *stuff,* a fair amount of it spilling out into the hallway. Riding the momentum of this wave of random goods and bric-a-brac, Neth was propelled into the hallway as well, sliding to a gentle stop just shy of the opposite wall.

"Wow!" exclaimed Hops. "Is this all your stuff?"

"I think," said Neth, "that this is *everyone's* stuff,

everyone who owns a Bag of Holding."

"Are there any bananas in there?" asked the rabbit, standing on his hind legs and examining the mound more carefully.

"Forget about food! Now's our chance to get out of here!" declared Neth, sheathing his new sword and scooping up Hops. "I just hope we can get out the way you got in."

"But what about the others?" asked Hops. "There's a big, heavy door at the end of this hallway. I'll bet it leads to the dungeon, and that's probably where they are!"

"Good, they can rot there for all I care!" growled Neth. "Those jerkholes are why we're in this mess in the first place!" He was already striding down the hall in the opposite direction.

"I know Yeth is a hothead and Dergar is kind of a tool," Hops said sadly, "but Noe and Brother Thelonious are nice. I like them." There was a funny feeling in Neth's stomach that he did his best to ignore. "Besides," Hops continued, "isn't this what we wanted? An adventure?"

Neth sighed. His pace slowed. He stopped.

"Where did you say this door was?" he grumbled.

"Hooray!" said Hops.

19

YOU CAN'T HAVE A DUNGEON
WITHOUT A DRAGON

"So... she's *eating* them?"

"Apparently," said Hops. The stairs they found behind the big, heavy door seemed to descend forever, so Neth and Hops had plenty of time to compare notes. And, like the rest of the castle, it was made of dirty ice, so Neth was happy that it was a proper stairwell and not open stairs, right up to the point where the left wall fell away and they found themselves staring down, down, down... into the largest underground chamber Neth had ever seen. Hops was already hugging the right wall.

"You could put a pool table in there and never worry about your cue hitting a wall," the rabbit nervously quipped.

"I never know what you're talking about..." said Neth.

A pale, unnatural light rose from the bottom of the enormous chamber, and as the two of them got closer to the foot of the stairs Neth could discern a large, dark... something... resting in the middle of the floor. "It's a dragon," whispered Hops. Neth froze.

"What?" he stage whispered.

"It's a dragon," Hops repeated. "My eyes are better

than yours in the dark. I can see him." Neth squinted at the shadowy mountain of an object just below them now, and he thought that, yes, he could see it slowly rising and falling, as if it were breathing. "It's asleep," Hops continued, carefully peeping over the edge of the stairs and examining the shape. "And it's chained to the floor with big steel manacles. There's a manacle around its mouth too."

"We are way out of our league, here," Neth groaned.

"I'm also seeing a heavy wooden door on the far wall," Hops continued, ignoring him. Tilting his head, the rabbit repositioned his ears several times, as if he were trying to tune in to a stubborn radio station.

"Must you always be so theatrical?" sighed Neth.

"The acoustics are weird in here," Hops explained. "There! I can hear them! They're definitely behind that door!"

"Are they being tortured?" Neth asked, in the manner that one might inquire about the health of a complete stranger.

"They're arguing," said Hops.

20

THE NOT-SO-GREAT ESCAPE

"I am not a proud man!" Dergar declared, pacing back and forth across the cell. "I can admit when I've made an error! And how could I not? My errors are all around me!" He gestured at the others for emphasis.

"You blame *us* for this misfortune?" asked Yeth, incredulous. "'Twas your plan from the first! You and your daft sovereign!'"

"Yes, my plan! My plan to press a base coward into service and then hire a dirty old man..."

"Guilty as charged," Brother Thelonious interjected.

"...and two fool dwarves to keep him in line!"

"Best watch who you call 'fool'," Yeth said, standing up.

"I can be excused for hiring you," Dergar continued, staring Yeth down. "At least you *look* like an adventurer, but what about this one?" Dergar pointed an accusing finger at Noe. "He doesn't even look like a *dwarf*, all fussy and clean-shaven! He looks like a goddamned gnome, or... or a brownie!"

"Best watch your tongue, man!" said Yeth, clenching his fists. "'Tis my blood of whom you speak!"

"No, you know what he looks like?" Dergar said

with a nasty smirk. "He looks like... a *hobbit*."

"That tears it!" shouted Yeth.

"Psst! Keep it down in there," hissed a voice from the other side of the cell door.

"Who dares?" huffed Dergar with all the pomposity he could muster. Neth held Hops' face up to the small, barred window set in the heavy door.

"Rescue rabbit!" chirped Hops.

"Listen, you nitwits," whispered Neth as the others gathered around the window. "There's a cartoonishly large padlock securing this door. Do any of you know where the key is?"

"Doubtless the witch has it on her person!" said Dergar.

"I can pick locks!" Noe offered.

"Okay," Neth said patiently through gritted teeth, "but you are on the *other side of the door*."

"Oh, yes," said Noe, frowning.

"I'm going to have to break it off then, but we need to make as little noise as possible *because there is a farking **dragon** out here*."

"Yes! A dragon we shall be seizing in the name of King Nomolos!" Dergar exclaimed.

"No!" snapped Neth. "We are not seizing any dragons or killing any witches or killing or fighting *anybody,* is that clear? We are in *way* over our heads here, so when I get this door open we are getting out of this castle and then putting as much distance between us and it as possible, got it?" Dergar mumbled something under his breath, but he didn't protest, so Neth took that as acquiescence. He turned his attention to the padlock. It was sturdy and looked nearly new. It wouldn't break easily. "I guess I'm gonna have to find a big rock or something and see if I can bash this thing off," he said. "I hope that dragon's a sound sleeper."

"'Give me a place to stand and I shall move the earth'," said Hops.

"What?" Neth said irritably. Hops sighed.

"Try using your sword as a pry bar. It'll make a lot less noise."

"Good idea," said Neth. Sliding the blade of his new sword through the shackle, he gave it a twist.

The sword cut through the lock like butter, and the severed lock fell to the icy floor with a dull metal clang. Neth and Hops stared in disbelief.

"Did you see that?" said Neth.

"Where did you get that sword?" asked Hops.

"I... found it on the floor."

"Really?"

"Really."

Shoving the others aside, Dergar was the first one out of the cell. "Those presumptuous popsicles relieved us of our weapons!" he blustered. "So our first duty is to re-arm ourselves! Then we'll begin a systematic search of the castle..."

"No," said Neth firmly. "What did I just say? You're no longer in charge of this farce, Dergar, so pipe down and listen. Our first goal is to get back upstairs without waking up this dragon. Fortunately, I've yet to see any of those animated snowmen Hops told me about, so maybe they're only posted near the entrances."

"Maybe she gave them the afternoon off to see the Ice Capades," suggested Hops.

"Zip it, rodent," Neth snapped. "Yeth, I want you to take the lead. That way we'll have a solid brawler at the front of the line. I'll go second because I'm currently the only one armed, plus I'm taller. Anyone comes at us, Yeth hits 'em low and I hit 'em high.

Dergar, you're our only other fighter so find something to use as a makeshift weapon and guard the rear." Grumbling, Dergar nevertheless cast his eyes about and eventually found what appeared to be an old fireplace poker that would serve the purpose. "Brother T and Noe, you guys are in the middle. Noe, I want you to carry Hops."

"Yes, sir!" said Noe cheerfully.

Favoring the left wall, they proceeded slowly upwards, their eyes repeatedly drawn, despite their best efforts, to the slumbering dragon below. Everyone breathed a sigh of relief when the tapered wall began to rise from the right side of the stairs and met the ceiling within a hundred steps, finally encasing them in the secure womb of a proper stairwell. Yet still they climbed in cautious silence, pausing, listening, each man or dwarf (or rabbit) occasionally realizing that he was holding his breath, inhaling deeply, and then, a few seconds later, realizing that he was holding his breath again. Finally, the door at the top of the stairs came into view, and a moment later they found themselves in the coldly sumptuous ice hallway. "So far, so good," whispered Neth.

"What now, fearless leader?" asked Yeth. There wasn't a hint of sarcasm in his voice.

"You and I will continue to take the point," Neth said. "Dergar, I want you to..." His face fell as he turned to address the captain of the guard. "For fark's sake," he groaned. "Where's Dergar?"

21

EVERYTHING GOES WRONG

Dergar had let the others get a little bit ahead of him, then, as they rounded a bend, turned tail and quickly retraced his steps back into the cavernous dungeon. Now, he stood before the great winged reptile that slumbered there, staring at it with self-righteous determination. He would *not* be derailed by the cowardice and base treachery of his companions. He would *not* return to his king in ignominious defeat. And, most importantly, he would *not* lose his quarterly performance bonus. Fortunately, he had a plan, and it began with freeing this dragon. If it was a Nogard dragon, it would instinctively return home, and he would make sure that he got all the credit for returning it. If it wasn't, well, it would still raise plenty of hell, distracting the witch princess and hopefully allowing him to get the drop on her.

He examined the enormous manacles that held the dragon's jaw shut and bound its feet to the floor. As he'd suspected, they were the same brand used back home, and they did not require a key. A dragon's claws were far too big to properly manipulate the mechanism that released the catch, but human hands could easily manage it. With a few deft twists, Dergar unlocked each set of manacles, freeing the dragon's rear legs first, then its front legs, and finally releasing the clamp that held its jaws shut. The dragon yawned and shifted in its sleep, taking unconscious advantage of its sudden increased freedom of motion, but did not awaken. Perfect. Dergar searched the floor until he found what he needed – a fist-sized chunk of ice, roundish in shape. Then, carefully skirting the slumbering creature, he made his way back up the stairs until he was looking down on the glorious creature a good hundred feet below. Taking a deep breath, he hauled back and hurled the chunk of ice at the dragon's face.

The dragon started as the ice bounced off the end of its nose. It slowly opened its huge golden eyes and cautiously lifted its head, quite baffled. Rising to its full height, it carefully opened and closed its jaw, cracked its neck, and examined its front feet, lifting each one in turn and flexing its toes, assuring itself that it was no longer bound. Then, alert to or at least suspecting a presence, its head darted about, shining eyes searching the far corners of the sizable chamber. But it didn't think to look up, and Dergar remained undiscovered. He smiled as a low rumble emanated from the dragon's throat. It was very, very angry. With a disdainful snort, it inhaled deeply, held its breath for just an instant – as if savoring the moment – and then let loose with a sweeping, devastating blast of flaming breath that engulfed the entirety of the dungeon, the lower half of the staircase, and the load-bearing foundations of the castle.

Load-bearing foundations, Dergar suddenly remembered, that were composed almost entirely of *ice*.

"Faaarkaaasssss!" he screamed, fleeing up the stairs.

* * *

"Did you... hear something?" asked Hops. So far, no one had attempted to hinder their escape, and now the archway that opened up into the main entrance hall was just ahead. The front doors, and freedom, were less than a hundred feet away. To their left, another wide, well-lit corridor led deeper into the castle. To their right, a set of stairs led upwards, into darkness. The stairs were the only place where an attacker could be hiding. Neth focused his attention there, listening carefully.

"No..." he began, only to be cut off by a horrific, all-encompassing grinding, like two glaciers trying to pass one another in a narrow hallway. The entire building canted forward, and suddenly the front doors were swept away by what appeared to be a reverse avalanche: a mixture of ice, sand, and slush that burst *upward,* out of the ground. Neth and the others backpedaled just in time, because now the entrance hall floor was *melting,* almost instantly dissolving into a thick, muddy soup. The walls and ceiling went next: cracking, losing their cohesion, and then collapsing entirely, effectively blocking their escape route. Just beyond, they sensed rather than saw something huge emerge from beneath the disintegrating floor as the dragon battered and melted its way out of the catacombs and took flight.

"We have to go back!" shouted Yeth. "We'll be buried alive!"

"Up, up the stairs!" ordered Neth. "Maybe we can jump out a window or something!"

"Jump out a window? *That's* your plan?" cried Brother Thelonious.

"If you've got a better idea, I'm all ears!" Neth called over his shoulder as he ran for the stairs.

99

"I'm all ears too!" Hops quipped.

"Not now!" Noe admonished the rabbit.

Neth cursed under his breath as they dashed up the steps. The stairwell, which curved gently to the left, seemed to go on forever and they were clearly ascending much more than a single story. Sure enough, when he reached the top he found himself on an open-air wall-walk high above the courtyard. Rushing to the edge and peering over the parapet, he confirmed his fears. It was much, much too high to jump. The rest of the party, spilling out of the doorway behind him, was far more engaged by the sight of the dragon. Now airborne, it was lazily circling the castle and systematically dousing its former prison with exhalations of organic plasma. As they watched, the monster inundated an entire tower with flame, reducing it in seconds to a slurry of steaming mud.

"Gods almighty, this couldn't possibly get any worse," Neth groaned.

*"Are you **fucking** serious right now???"* a woman screamed from the far end of the walkway.

"Oh yeah," sighed Neth. "The witch."

22

ENDGAME

Princess Skylar Skylark emerged from the tower at the opposite end of the walk, wearing nothing but a towel, her hair soaking wet, soap bubbles still clinging to her skin. The look on her face was a mixture of utter confusion and white-hot rage. *"What have you hooligans done?"* she shrieked. *"I just took out a second mortgage on this place!"* Punctuating this, the far wall of the castle broke down entirely and collapsed into a shapeless mound of mud. The dragon, apparently satisfied, was already winging its way off into the sunset. "You..." Skylar said coldly, pointing at Neth. "I'm going to kill *you* first. No one will *ever* die as horribly as you!"

The battlement chose this moment to partially give way, the wall below them buckling and tilting wildly towards the courtyard, throwing everyone to the floor. Everyone, that is, except Skylar, who was hurled into the melting parapets. Sinking into the thick mud of the liquefying barricade, she slowly began to slide *through* it and over the side of the wall. *"No! No!!!"* she screamed. Propelling himself so that he slid down the slick, canted walkway, Neth crashed into the tower wall behind her (his left foot went right through it) and grabbed the witch's ankle just before she went over the edge. "I meant what I said," Skylar snarled as he struggled to haul her up. "You're a marked man! Castration is only the beginning, I promise you!" Neth pulled her to safety anyway. She really was that hot.

"This changes nothing," she snarled, locking eyes with him. Yet, simultaneously, her hand found his and gave it a quick squeeze. What in the world did *that* mean?

"You've got her, swordsman!" boomed Dergar excitedly, climbing out of the first stairwell. He'd managed to arm himself with a poleaxe, which he used to herd the others in front of him as he advanced on Neth and Skylar. "Hold her down and I'll finish her off!"

"Nobody's getting finished off!" Neth said. "If you want to arrest her, fine, but I'm not letting you run someone through just because they poached a few dragons!" With great care, he climbed to his feet, drew his sword, and stepped around his friends. Dergar jabbed at him with his much longer weapon, once, twice, thrice, constantly keeping Neth on the defensive.

"Yon poleaxe has twice the reach!" lamented Yeth. "'Tis hardly a fair fight!"

"I don't fight fair," smiled Dergar, "I fight to win!" He lunged forward, plunging the tip of the poleaxe into his opponent's thigh. Neth fell to his knees, dropping his sword and crying out in pain.

"It's over! Stop!" shouted Brother Thelonious.

"It's over when I deliver the killing blow!" said Dergar, raising the poleaxe.

A white blur bounded up the wall, propelled itself off the parapet with its small but powerful legs, and landed on Dergar's shoulder. Hops sunk his incisors deep into Dergar's cheek.

"Wretched beast!" screamed Dergar, grabbing Hops by the neck and hurling him into the parapet with all his strength. The rabbit hit with a sickening crunch and the disintegrating parapet collapsed on top of him, burying him in mud. "Now..." he turned to Neth.

Neth, who had used this momentary distraction to retrieve his sword.

Neth, whose face was a mask of hate and rage.

Neth, who, in one smooth motion, stood, sidestepped Dergar's panicky thrust, and effortlessly plunged his sword into the man's right eye – right up to the hilt – and out the back of his skull.

"Urk," said Dergar. It would serve as his epitaph, for he was quite dead.

"You did it!" cheered Noe.

And then the castle fell down.

Much to everyone's surprise, the castle's final bow was a rather controlled affair, for all that: essentially a brief, unspectacular mudslide that the party rode to the ground with only minor injuries, most of these incurred by collisions with furniture and other weighty items mixed in with the slop. Wiping the muck from his eyes, Neth carefully sat up. Not far away, Noe's feet stuck straight up out of the mud, kicking wildly. Yeth, Brother Thelonious, and the girl were okay too. Yeth hadn't even lost his helmet. But where was Hops? With a horrible, sinking feeling in the pit of his stomach Neth cast about, trying to figure out where the rabbit might have come to ground. Finally, spying a lump that *could* have once been the parapet that had fallen on Hops, he desperately began to dig. And, under several inches of suffocating mud, he found the bunny. Neth pulled the limp form free. "He's not breathing! *He's not breathing!*" he cried. *"What do you do when someone's not breathing? Someone tell me, please! Someone help him!"* The others gathered around, but no one spoke for nearly a minute as Neth rocked back and forth, cradling the lifeless rabbit to his chest. "Someone help him..." he repeated over and over again. Yeth, with great reverence, removed his helmet and held it over his heart.

"He died a hero, Swordsman," said the dwarf gently. "In truth, the rodent was as brave – braver – than any dwarf I have e'er known."

"He wasn't a rodent," Neth said quietly. "He was a *lagomorph.*"

23

EPILOGUESQUE

"So you were *eating* the dragons?" Noe asked, incredulous. "Why?" Skylar, still wrapped in a towel, was wrenching one of her bureau drawers free of the clinging mud. She wanted to put on some proper clothes, but, naturally, the drawer she'd salvaged contained only underwear. She wasn't going to walk around in only her skivvies: she wasn't some sexist pulp novel cliché.

"Well," she said, in answer to Noe's question, "in all honesty it started out as a fad diet that kind of got out of hand." Frowning at her wardrobe options, Skylar looked up just in time to see Brother Thelonious carrying the dead rabbit away from their impromptu campsite. He'd offered to bury Hops and say a short prayer over the grave. Neth, who couldn't bring himself to participate, was morosely stirring the campfire, his thoughts his own. The old cleric looked furtively over his shoulder, and then disappeared behind the mountain of drying mud that used to be her castle. Skylar decided to follow him.

"Is it hard to make a castle out of ice?" Noe was asking. Skylar dismissed him with a wave of her hand.

"I'll be right back," she said.

"What are you up to, old man?"

"Just considering what I'm about to do," he said, gently laying the rabbit on the ground in front of him. "It's probably not a very good idea."

"What's not a very good idea?"

"I didn't want to get Neth's hopes up," he confided, "but it is within my power, theoretically, to raise the recently deceased. At the discretion of my patron deity, of course." The cleric frowned. "In this case, however, the goddess I follow may find the request quite insulting. There could be... consequences."

"Why insulting?"

"Well," Brother Thelonious said, "it's a *rabbit*."

"But it talks, right? That's got to be good for some celestial credit."

"I certainly hope so. You might want to take a step back, in case I'm instantly struck down by lightning." Skylar smiled at his joke. "I'm not kidding," he said. She took two steps back.

Raising his hands to the sky, Brother Thelonious began to chant.

"If you're going to stir something, stir this!" said Yeth, placing a large kettle of brownish goop on the fire. "It's lizard and sagebrush stew, and don't complain because we're lucky to have that!" Yeth waited for a response. When he didn't get one, he continued. "We'll break camp in the morning and return the way we came. Once we reach the Pleasant Hills we can go our separate ways."

Neth nodded absently.

"It's settled then," said Yeth. "The witch – excuse me, the *sorceress* – has offered to accompany us that far at least. She should come in very handy in facing the dangers ahead."

"Okay," Neth said absently. Yeth took a deep breath. This wouldn't do. The man would have to snap out of it. "Listen to me..." he began.

"Swordsman!" Skylar's voice broke in. "Someone would have words with you!"

Neth looked up. Skylar and Brother Thelonious stood before him, the latter holding Hops. Hops, bright eyed, nose wiggling, very, very much alive.

"Hops!" Neth shouted as the rabbit leapt out of the cleric's arms and into his own. He pulled him close and squeezed him as tight as he dared.

"Wait until I tell you what Rabbit Heaven is like!" Hops said.

"Hops..." is all Neth said in response. He shut his eyes tight to keep the tears in, and it almost worked.

"You've done a wonderful thing, old man," Skylar whispered to Brother Thelonious. "But would you kindly remove your hand from my ass?"

"Of course," the cleric said, acquiescing.

"Okay!" Skylar clapped her hands. "Now, let's get to work! You all owe me one castle!"

"How much does a magic castle cost?" asked Noe.

"If you let Neth cut your head off, he can contribute five thousand silver pieces," suggested Brother Thelonious.

"That wouldn't even cover the heating bill," said Skylar.

It wasn't very funny, but everyone laughed, because when everyone laughs at a bad joke, poorly told, that's a lazy storytelling device letting you know that it is, indeed,

THE END

ABOUT THE AUTHOR

Brad D. Sibbersen is probably not a rabbit.

Also by Brad D. Sibbersen:

Welcome to Mad Science U

Deadburbia

The World That Time Forgot

Demons & Dragons

Everything Bad Happens to Jeremiah Riddle

Brought to Rune

Involuntary

Graves Not Deep Enough

Dead Fall

Road Works: Four Tales

Amityville Subdivision

The Faerie Pit

Bombed

Look What's Happened to Mad Science U